ISBN-13: 978-1-952412-02-8

Cover design: Christopher Doll

Published By: Vagabond Publishing

Library of Congress Control Number: 1952412021

Printed in the United States of America

CONTENTS

The *Vagabond* rattled and jerked every few seconds as the braking thrusters fired to slow the ship on its approach to Luna. Erik Frost, captain and owner of the guild freighter, gripped the padded armrests of his command chair at every sudden movement. Despite living on the ship through his teen years and returning to lead the small crew after his father's unexpected death four years before, Erik could never shake the feeling that the ship was going to tear itself apart during every acceleration or braking burn. For the thousandth time, he promised himself to do a full refit of the old freighter at the Luna shipyards. As soon as he had the creds to afford it, that is, which would be many years in the future at the rate his finances were running.

Eyes darting across the holographic displays in front of him, Erik checked the hull integrity and cargo bay integrity readouts to find them sitting at the usual percentages. Neither was as high as he'd like them to be, but they were well within a safe range. The ship would survive this trip, his seventh guild run as captain. His white-knuckle grip relaxed as the thrusters began to fire in shorter and less powerful bursts, and the ship calmed to the steady throbbing he was more accustomed to.

"We've attained orbital velocity, Captain," the *Vagabond*'s pilot announced. John Murphy, a graying veteran of the shipping lanes, had served as pilot of the ship for a decade and a half. An old friend of Erik's father, he had joined the crew before it left Earth and seemed content to make it his home until his last days.

"How long until our berth is ready?" Erik asked, looking to his left where he saw the back of the pilot's station.

"Aurora has us landing in a little over five hours," he replied.

Releasing the restraints that kept him secured in the command chair during the burn, Erik stretched out the kinks in his muscles and keyed the intercom. "Five hours, folks. Let's make sure everything is shipshape and ready for the arrival inspections. Tuya, meet me in the bay and we'll double check the cargo."

With the ship under a light thrust providing only half of Earth's gravity, Erik felt as if he almost floated as he moved to the door of the control room at the heart of the vessel. He continued his graceful light-footed pace as he traversed the corridors forward to the vast cargo bay that occupied a third of the *Vagabond*.

The bay was large enough to haul up to half a dozen of the thousand-ton capacity cargo pods that the mining colonies used to receive supplies or send out loads of ores and minerals dredged up from the asteroids or moons they inhabited. At the moment, the freighter was carrying only one of the massive pods, with thirty smaller containers they were being paid to deliver to the home world via the Transport Guild hub on Luna.

The captain entered the bay's starboard side, gratified to see that his cargo specialist was already checking the webbing that kept the containers tight to the deck. Tuya Sansar's diminutive five-foot frame meant that she was often overlooked by those who did not know her, but the cybernetic enhancements throughout her body gave her a strength that was hard to believe until witnessed. It always came as a surprise to those who chose to cross her, since the enhancements were illegal throughout the system and always came with significant drawbacks when purchased on the black market.

"How's everything looking?" Erik called out as he moved across the room to join her at the control screen for the cargo pod.

"The containers are secure, and the webbing hasn't shifted an inch since we left Deimos." Tuya focused on the controls in front of her as she punched in commands to pull up an overview of the contents of the pod that towered over her, four times as tall as she was and more than thirty meters in length. She cycled through various screens as her eyes quickly scanned and found the relevant data. "The pod is secure, as well, and the contents have experienced only minor shifting. Well within limits."

"That's great news. This old ship shakes so much sometimes that I feel like everything must be rolling around in here."

Tuya shot her captain a skeptical glance with a raised eyebrow. "Frost, the day any of my cargo 'rolls around', as you call it, you have my permission to fire me and bring in someone who hasn't obviously gone senile."

Erik flashed a smile and reached out a fist to bump her shoulder. "No way I'd want to get rid of you, Tuya." His father had run the ship with a crew of five and handled the cargo himself, but Erik had brought in a sixth crewmember as soon as he took over so he could focus on the ship and crew as a whole. He would never replace any of the old crew, and thought of them all as family. Tuya had fit in well with the group from the outset, maintaining the cohesive feel onboard.

The cargo specialist returned the smile briefly, and then turned back to the display in front of her. She got along well with her captain, but had sometimes wondered if her hire had been more about youthful infatuation than her experience and skills; she knew that her Asiatic features were appealing to both sexes, and had to fight off more advances that she had ever wanted to receive. Those thoughts came to her less and less over the years as Frost showed her nothing but respect and friendship. The *Vagabond* had become her home, and she increasingly felt accepted into the fraternity of the crew.

"I'll run a few diagnostics to make sure nothing inside the pod or containers has been damaged during transit. If anything comes up, I'll send you an alert right away."

Erik nodded once, and with a pat on her shoulder he glided across the cargo bay toward the port hatch. At the door, he paused to turn back and look over the cavernous space, the worn metal lit intermittently by lights inset in the walls two meters above the floors and below the high dome-like ceiling. The walls curved gently toward the bow, where two large doors opened to allow for loading and unloading cargo. It was hard for him to remember now why leaving the ship and joining the Coalition navy had seemed so important when he reached eligibility at seventeen.

With a wistful smile, he shouldered open the hatch and then pushed it closed behind him before moving aft through the narrow corridor toward the reactor room. Passing the combined lab and med bay on the anterior side of the corridor, he glanced in to find them unsurprisingly empty. Sally Murphy was the best ship's doctor he'd ever met, devoted to the health of her crew and equally devoted to her husband John. He had no doubt she had joined the pilot in the control center as soon as she could leave her crash couch.

Entering the reactor room, the captain cast his eyes toward the radiation meter. Aside from a Coalition frigate destroyed by Syndicate-sponsored sabotage during a brief flare up in the cold war when he was a young boy, it had been more than three decades since the last reactor accident that flooded a ship with radiation. But caution around the nuclear power plant was one of the first things a person learned when joining a ship's crew. It was ingrained early and often. There were always rumors swirling around about some fantastical new power source being developed in a secret lab somewhere, but nuclear fission had always been the most reliable and economical source of power for space travel and the far-flung colonies. Seeing that the radiation levels were normal, he popped the hatch and entered the territory of the ship's engineer.

Fynn Jesperson was a third-generation spacefarer, hailing from a family that had been among the earliest corporation-backed astronauts, pre-cursors of the Corporate Syndicate that was now one of the two major political powers on Earth. The old Norwegian had spent two thirds of his life serving aboard ships like the *Vagabond*, drawn to the mysteries of the engine room from the moment he set foot aboard his first ship. Erik found the engineer stooped over the main console in the center of the room, monitoring some esoteric bit of the engine or reactor. The freighter had one of the lowest repair rates among the Transport Guild ships, all thanks to the careful ministrations of Jesperson.

"How's it going, Fynn? She sounds pretty smooth right now."

Owlish eyes were turned toward the captain, a mixture of surprise and consternation evident upon being interrupted in his musings. "Oh, it's you! Sorry I didn't hear you come in, Erik, I was just having another look through my girl's stats. She's purring like a kitten for us today." He reached out and affectionately patted the nearest bulkhead that covered parts of the engines. The crew often speculated on whether the engineer loved anything as much as the inner workings of the ship he lived in.

"That's great to hear," the young captain said. He glanced around the room a bit sheepishly as he considered whether to ask what was on his mind. "Say, did the shaking during the braking burn seem worse than usual to you? Anything we could do to cut down on that?"

A glower that Erik remembered well from his younger years was turned upon him. "Erik, you know very well that my engines are not responsible for the decrepit body that surrounds them. The shaking is harmless, as I've told you countless times before, and will continue until our hull and internal structure can be reworked and reinforced."

Erik held out a conciliatory hand, regretting the question even as it had left his mouth. "I'm not blaming you at all, Fynn. I'm hoping we'll have the creds to do a hull refit in three or four years. I just wish there was some kind of jury rigging we could do to make things easier on my nerves."

Satisfied that his integrity was not being called into question, the Norwegian relaxed the glowering stare and his eyes slowly took on the glaze of deep thought. "There have been times I thought about adjusting our old stabilizers, moving them to different parts of the ship to see if it might carry the load better." The engineer turned away and began walking away from his captain, lost in thought. "Or perhaps if we fired the thrusters for a longer interval with slightly less power behind them..."

Erik sheepishly rubbed the back of his head and wondered how long his engineer would be off on a tangent thinking about theoretical fixes for something that seemingly was only a problem for him. It was such an irrational concern, but yet he had never talked himself out of it when the rattling and shaking started.

Leaving the reactor room, Erik continued his journey through the looping corridor of the ship and checked in on the common areas as he returned to the command center. The galley and rec room were on the opposite anterior edge from the medical and scientific area. Both were worn but clean, with anything that could have been dislodged in the braking maneuver locked away in cabinets and drawers. The crew quarters lining the interior side of the corridor were all locked down, and anything left loose there was the responsibility of the occupant. The crew used five of the eight small cabins on board, and on rare occasions would rent out a room to a passenger that didn't mind the sparse accommodations.

Near the end of the loop around the ship, he passed the technology hub and heard the faint murmuring of the ship's technician, Isaac Szymanski, chatting with the AI interface. The bearded self-proclaimed computer geek kept the AI running smoothly and maintained the many miles of fiber optic cables running through the ship that kept the computer connected with every system on board. Erik sometimes thought the man had allowed the ship's AI to advance a little too far towards true sentience, but appreciated the increased efficiency that resulted.

Re-entering the command center, Erik saw Sally and John with their heads together at the pilot station. Sally smiled over at the captain before turning back to the conversation with her husband. He returned to his crash couch and pulled up the holographic displays to check the status of their docking platform. He keyed the ship's intercom, announcing "Three hours left until descent. Make sure the shopping lists are updated and ready to go. We'll have two days in port before we head out for the mining colony on Interamnia."

The sprawling but still small settlement on the surface of Luna began as a collection of inflatable habitat domes linked together. The colony was close to the Apollo 11 landing site, allowing the inhabitants to look out tiny windows to view the historic lander that began humanity's slow outward expansion; it was a replica of the Eagle, with a flag nearby that had been whitewashed by solar radiation.

With its reduced gravity and almost non-existent atmosphere, the corporations quickly realized that Luna was the best place to build a shipyard and docking platforms for their spacecraft. Earth's governments had fallen behind in their efforts to explore and colonize beyond the home world, leaving a gap for the fabulously rich CEOs of multi-national corporations to fill as they pursued their dreams of blazing new trails and creating legacies that could last for centuries.

Two low domes were built over the years to contain the modest population of Earth's moon, each named for one of the first two people to set foot on Luna's surface. Armstrong dome was completed in 2038 by the corporation-backed explorers. It was capable of housing more than a thousand people and connected to the small number of docking platforms on the northern edge of Mare Tranquillitatis. Developed nations banded together to form a political counterpart to the mega-rich corporations, and Aldrin dome was constructed nearby seven years later to establish the newly christened Coalition presence, encompassing twice as much of the lunar surface with the capacity for three times as many citizens. They had made plans through the years for more domes, but the stagnant policies of the cold war resulted in maintaining the status quo.

The domes were connected via a half-mile-long tunnel, built for motorized and pedestrian traffic flow. At the start of hostilities between the Coalition and the Syndicate, a corporate conglomeration that had purchased several poor countries to run as they saw fit, in 2052, checkpoint stations were erected to control access to each of the domes. For years the tunnel remained almost deserted as each group prevented entry into the domes for fear of saboteurs and spies.

As the war between the superpowers dragged on with only petty skirmishes for more than a decade and became a tense stalemate, the restrictions were loosened. Those willing to undergo strenuous background checks and sit in sterile government offices for hours on end waiting to answer a few hundred seemingly nonsensical questions were sometimes granted passes allowing for transit between the Coalition- and Syndicate-controlled domes.

Erik Frost, like most of the guild freighter captains, had gone through the torturous process, and therefore crossed between domes with near impunity. He stood impatiently at the entry checkpoint for Aldrin, watching the Coalition guards double and triple check his pass. The *Vagabond* had been docked on the Armstrong pads this trip, necessitating the transit between domes since the Syndicate refused to allow a guild office in their domain. The young guardswoman scowled at him as she gave up on finding reasons to prevent his entry, and almost threw the pass back at him before gesturing him through the electronic barrier.

Walking through the small city toward the guildhall in the central marketplace, Erik marveled once more at how different the two domes were. While the older Syndicate dome was built for comfort and had wide avenues and a scattering of small park squares, the newer and larger Coalition dome was built with utilitarian construction to cram more people into the space and maximize scientific and manufacturing spaces. The marketplace at the heart of Aldrin was the only area in the dome that looked appealing to the young captain's eyes, with a handful of airy shops surrounding a small plaza where colonists would gather to socialize in free time.

The Transport Guildhall was a long, low building that dominated one side of the plaza. It was built of the same bland gray lunar dust concrete as the other buildings around it, but draped on the walls were small colorful flags denoting the symbols and ship names of each captain who belonged to the guild. Erik quickly counted the flags, seeing nineteen with the *Vagabond*'s flag on the top row. One more than his last trip through Luna, which meant a new crew competing for shipping contracts with the six modest colonies in the asteroid belt and the smaller outpost on the Martian moon of Deimos.

Established shortly before the long cold war between the superpowers began, the guild had picked up jobs transporting goods throughout the inner system. Business increased as the Coalition and Syndicate focused on the production of warships at the expense of cargo haulers, and instead paid fees to independent captains with their own ships. The guild remained a neutral entity, working with either of the Earth powers.

The move had kick-started a flurry of repairs as out-of-service ships were salvaged from scrapyards to retrofit, overhaul, or just do basic repairs on them and get the ship flying to earn credits. More than half of those early ships had gone missing in the vastness of space, presumed lost to malfunctions or micro meteor impacts on frail hull plating.

Erik's father had dreamed of joining those pioneers of the stars for almost a decade before he found an old decommissioned ore hauler that had been within his budget. Two years were spent repairing and upgrading the *Vagabond* before they had been able to launch from Earth to join the shipping lanes.

Inside the bustling hall was a row of desks with low walls between them for a modicum of privacy. At the far end of the hall was the single office, comfortably but sparsely decorated and occupied by the president of the guild. The occupants of most of the desks were busy chatting via video feeds with clients or captains, maintaining the ever growing web of shipping activities overseen by the guild. Erik saw that the representative he usually dealt with was not occupied, and hurried over to take a seat in front of the battered old desk.

"Hey, Dex, how's it going?"

The young woman at the desk looked up from a tablet she was perusing and smirked at the captain, amber eyes shining with mischief. "I heard some claptrap pretending to be a ship had landed at the Armstrong docks. Survived another trip in that old tin can, huh?"

"I like to make sure we're recognizable so my favorite guild rep always knows when I've arrived," he said with a wink.

Dexterity Avila smiled wider, flashing even white teeth. "What wonders have you brought back with you from this trip, Frost?"

"We picked up the pod from Hygeia. The miners there are asking for an extra shipment of fuel rods, by the way. The foreman said that they've hit a hard rock layer between mineral deposits that's using up more power than expected. I put the paperwork in my upload when we docked." Dex nodded and made a note of the request for the next shipment sent out to the colony. "The colony on Davida appreciated that container of heavy fabric we'd been hauling around for eight months, said it was perfect for creating their own work gear instead of buying in pre-made stuff at a higher price. The outpost on Deimos had a load of thirty containers that need to be delivered to the Syndicate on Earth. Sounds like their scientists on Mars are shipping back all the samples they've collected and examined over the last year, to be processed in the labs at home."

The representative's dark curls fell forward and she looked down at her tablet to check items off a list and send requests to have the cargo offloaded from the *Vagabond*.

"The pod and containers are scheduled for extraction in the overnight shift," she said. Erik watched her scroll through screen after screen, knowing she was looking at all the shipping requests that the guild was trying to get filled. "It looks like we already have you down to deliver an empty pod to Interamnia?"

"Yeah, I jumped on that job as soon as I saw it on the guild job list. I got a message from a researcher I know there asking me to swing by next time I was out in the belt."

"Getting paid to make a friendly visit, huh?" Dex asked with a grin.

"That's the guild way," Erik said.

"Lucky for you, we also have a small shipment of protein packs and freeze-dried fruits that need to go that way. I'll add the consignment to your job list, and get the containers loaded." She continued scrolling through the screen, and then paused to consider something. Looking up at Erik, she narrowed her eyes, "How would you feel about dropping some cargo at a black site?"

The captain sat up straight in his chair, eyes going wide. Black sites were locations set up to mine extremely valuable materials. According to rumor, they were also sometimes used to stockpile weapons and fuel rods to supply exploration vessels that would soon be going beyond the asteroid belt. Their existence was a poorly guarded secret, but the exact location of the small number of sites was something only a very few were privileged to know. As a result, the pay for the jobs was much higher than usual to make up for the increased risk.

"Do you think he'd really let me have a job like that?" Erik asked, nodding his head in the direction of the guild president's office. He had only met the guild's leader once very briefly, and knew that captains with the longest tenure were usually selected for such important jobs.

Dex shrugged and glanced over at the closed office door. "I know he trusted your father more than almost any other captain, and gave him a few of these kinds of jobs even before you left the ship to join the Coalition navy. The details are locked behind about a thousand layers of encryption, but if the projections are right it's only a month or so added on to your current route." She quickly typed in a permission request to assign the job and sent it off. Within a minute, her tablet pinged with a response.

"Well?" Erik asked, beginning to feel excited at the thought of such a job and the pay that would come with it. Perhaps it would be enough to cover all the debts left behind by his father.

"You're cleared for the job," the guild rep told him. "The caveat is that only your AI will be allowed to know the coordinates. You'll have to turn over navigation of the ship after you depart from Interamnia."

Erik considered that new bit of information, hesitant at the thought of not having control of his ship for a trip that would take at least a month. Noticing the hesitation, Dex shifted her tablet just enough for him to be able to see the proposed payment for the job. The numbers shown on the screen quickly overcame his hesitance.

"Sign us up. I think I can trust Aurora to be the pilot for that kind of pay." The job was quickly added to his ship's log and the load was assigned to be delivered to his cargo bay.

"Looks like that's all we have available for now, unless you want to start making long detours to colonies on the far side of the system."

"As much as I love being out in the black, I don't think I want to add that much time before I return. I have to see my favorite rep, after all." Erik tried out his most charming smile, eliciting a laugh from the woman across the desk.

"Sweet talk me all you want, captain, just don't expect any special favors." Dex flashed a wink and returned her gaze to the tablet. "Now it's time for your favorite representative to get back to work and try to meet her quotas. Have a great trip."

"Yes, ma'am," Erik replied, throwing a quick salute as he stood. A part of him was disappointed that his minor flirtation hadn't elicited a more encouraging response, but after several years of hopeless attempts he was content with the idea that Dex did not return his romantic interest. An inner voice yelled at him to be more up front about his feelings and ask the woman out for a date, but his shyness overruled the impulse.

Departing the guild hall, Erik took a short stroll around the airy shops. The rest of the crew was picking up the supplies they would need for the long voyage, but he liked to browse through the items being displayed and relax his mind for a while. Most shops in the square sold locally produced goods priced for the many tourists who loved to spend a few days in the intimate luxurious hotels in both domes. There was a small shop with baskets of hydroponic fruits and vegetables on display, the earthy smell of the freshly picked lettuce, tomatoes and herbs causing him to close his eyes and enjoy memories of his childhood spent on Earth. He had only set foot on the home world twice since the *Vagabond* left the planet, once when he joined the navy and again when he was discharged after learning of his father's death during a long haul through the asteroid belt.

Walking through the narrow streets back to the transit tunnel, he noticed more Coalition soldiers wandering the district than usual, their light armor plating worn tightly strapped over light gray uniforms. Each of them carried the standard non-lethal stun pistol, but he noticed that some guards were also carrying flechette rifles. Erik had never seen the lethal weapons being carried in a civilian setting. During the five years he served aboard a frigate, the rifles had been removed from the secure weapon lockers only once, when a Syndicate shuttle crashed in Coalition territory on Earth and sparked fears of renewed hostilities. The sight of the weapons now made him wonder what event had precipitated such action.

He considered asking the guards at the transit tunnel barrier, but they all still carried the glowers that invited him to fuck right off when he even glanced in their direction. Keeping his head down, Erik strode quickly away through the tunnel. He tried to pull up a news feed on his tablet, but the no-man's-land between the two domes was infamous for having no signal. Especially for the older technology of the physical tablets that most people still carried. Those who could afford the expensive holographic implants, which created a display over the eyeball that was visible as no more than a blue haze, often bragged of being able to pull data from almost anywhere in the system since the implants operated on a different signal wavelength that was much more powerful and projected farther. It was yet another item on the list of things the young captain wanted to splurge on if he was ever rolling in credits.

Arriving at the Syndicate checkpoint and noticing that the handful of guards there appeared to be in a better mood, he mentioned the weaponry he had seen and asked about it.

"Some kook tried to assassinate their Prime Minister," the guardsman told him with a chuckle. "He didn't even get close to succeeding, but they tried to say the Syndicate was behind the attack. All the evidence is pointing to the guy being one of those 'bring back the old world' cultist types, though. Now everyone over there," with a nod in the direction of Aldrin "is riled up and they seem to think an attack is imminent."

Erik glanced uncomfortably down the tunnel in the direction he had come from. He could only hope that cooler heads would prevail. The guards waved him through with only a perfunctory check, and he entered the airy confines of Armstrong with a heavy heart. Some freighter captains loved the idea of a full-out war, claiming that it would only boost profits for all the guild members, but Erik knew just how hard the Earth powers could clamp down on the sparsely populated system if they did so. The independent freighters could be put under heavy restrictions, making it impossible to afford the upkeep of the ships.

Returning to the docking platform corridors, he was happy to see that the Syndicate soldiers he passed along the way were only carrying standard weaponry. It relieved him to think the incident would not spark the conflagration of war. Especially when he had just accepted a job to deliver cargo to one of the most secretive locations in the system.

Two

Erik stumbled into the galley early the next morning, following the smell of freshly brewed coffee. It was the good stuff, too, that they were only able to indulge in while docked, instead of the instant coffee that provided a caffeine fix but tasted like bitter water. After a late night helping to oversee the offload of goods and the delivery of the first new load, he had managed only a few hours of sleep before his alarm pulled him out of blissful dreams. The temptation to stay in the comfortable cocoon of his bunk was only resisted with the thought that he could sleep in during the long flight out to the belt. There was too much to be done before they left to allow the luxury now.

"Good morning, captain," a gentle feminine voice said.

"Good morning, Aurora," he replied, sipping at the hot drink. "How are things today?"

"This ship is running at 83% efficiency," the AI responded. It was a number that would have caused palpitations in a military captain, but Erik had never seen the old freighter's efficiency higher than 87%. The ship had served as a cargo hauler between Earth and

Luna for more than a decade before his father rescued it from the scrapyard and cobbled together repairs with Fynn Jesperson and John Murphy.

"Any messages from the guild?" Erik asked, always hoping to get one more contract added on before leaving for a trip.

"We have received no messages, captain. I will route them to you with high priority should something come in."

"Thank you, Aurora."

"Miss. Sansar would like to see you in the cargo bay at your earliest opportunity, captain. Shall I tell her you are on the way now?"

"Yes, Aurora." Erik smiled at how pushy his AI could sometimes be, and shuffled his way to the cargo bay. The cargo specialist had been up with him until the early hours, so he was surprised that she was already hard at work. He wondered if she had bothered getting bunk time at all.

"Aurora said you wanted to see me?" he called out as he entered the poorly lit bay, looking over the large cargo pod that was destined for the mining colony on Interamnia. Making his way around the massive obstacle, he came to a stop when confronted with an oddly shaped container half the length but twice the width of a normal smoothly rounded cargo pod.

Tuya was leaning against the container, arms crossed, her lips a tight line of frustration. "What in the hell is this thing, Frost, and why wasn't I told to expect delivery of it?"

"Uh, did the details of the jobs I accepted not make it through to your tablet?" Erik was a little perplexed, since the details should have routed through the ship computer to the cargo specialist within seconds. Her priority level for alerts about new cargo was as high as his.

"Oh, I got notifications, all right. But this behemoth taking up half my cargo bay was not on that list." Tuya stepped forward and shoved her tablet in his face, a finger pointing at the alert details prominently displayed on the screen. The two jobs for Interamnia were listed, but nothing about the side trip to the black site location.

"That's for a third job I took on, but I guess the security level on it is high enough to override our internal alerts." He walked over to a small display on the front of the navy blue trapezoid container, tapping once to wake the display. His brows furrowed as the screen came alive but displayed only two words: CONSOLE LOCKED. He tapped it a few times experimentally, but nothing happened.

"I get the same thing," Tuya said. "The grunts who delivered this thing refused to say a word, and I'm almost certain they would have forcefully moved me if I had tried to block their access into the bay. What have you gotten us involved in?"

"Trust me, this job was way too good to pass up. The credits we'll get on delivery are enough to pay everyone's salary for a year and still have some left over."

"No one pays that much, Frost. No one reputable, anyway."

Erik shrugged, and turned to walk away. "It's a black site," he almost whispered.

Tuya narrowed her eyes and glared at her captain's back, her body going still and stiff. "Have you lost your mind?" she hissed. When he turned with wide eyes, she stalked forward and pushed him against a wall. "Do you have any idea how dangerous those places are? There is a reason the locations have never been leaked. They don't let anyone who finds them escape to spread the word."

"These contracts have come through the guild before," Erik protested. "They only provide location information to the ship's AI, and Aurora will navigate to the destination and back out again without any of us knowing a thing."

"You better hope so."

Anger sparked in the amber eyes boring into him. He'd always known that Tuya's temper could flare up in stressful situations, but he had never seen her as incensed as she was at that moment. He tried to think of ways to allay her fears, but the diminutive woman turned sharply and strode out of the cargo bay, the hatch slamming forcefully behind her. Erik rubbed at his shoulder, trying to take solace in the thought of the big payday that was to come. Surely all those credits would soothe any troubled feelings that remained after the long trip to the asteroid belt.

System Standard Time was established early in the era of the corporate explorers, based on the time zone where the majority of the billionaires funding them had resided. It was late evening according to that clock when the last of the containers being delivered to Interamnia were loaded on the *Vagabond*.

The ship's supplies had been replenished earlier in the day while most of the crew were enjoying a day off to visit the entertainment options of Luna. The engineer and technician returned with alcohol levels that would lead to hangovers and grumbling the next day. Meanwhile, the Murphys had passed time with a picnic and lounging in the park at the center of Armstrong dome. Botanists had managed to grow a few oak and cedar trees that residents and visitors loved to spend time around. Low gravity had allowed the trunks to grow tall and the branches to spread out much farther than they could on Earth. For those who lived in ships covered in metals and plastics, the chance to lie in green grass and watch branches full of leaves waving in a very gentle breeze was priceless.

Erik had not seen his cargo specialist since the argument in the bay, and checked with Aurora several times through the day to see if she was still on board. He kept trying to come up with a reason for her response to the trip, but was unsuccessful. The crew had reacted with surprise and hesitation when he caught them all in the galley at the same time to break the news, but none of them showed any anger at all. He decided to pursue the matter later on during the journey, when Tuya was ready to communicate with him again.

Luna cleared the ship for departure before midnight, and Erik watched from his crash couch in the control center as John keyed in the commands to retract the docking collar and gently launch from the platform. Both men watched as the gray pitted surface of Earth's moon slowly receded below them. Seeing both of the domes highlighted in the light of the sun peeking from behind Earth was awe inspiring, as was the view of a home world that both men had rarely set foot on. The lights of sprawling overcrowded cities glittered on the dark side of the planet facing them.

Answering a chime from his tablet, Erik saw a quick note had been sent to him via the guild servers. "Have a great trip. Come see me again when you're back at the domes. Dex." He smiled at the thought that the guild representative had been watching closely enough to know when *Vagabond* departed. Perhaps he should screw up the courage to ask her out when they returned to Luna, after all.

"Ten minutes to acceleration burn," John announced via the ship's intercom system. "We'll be under a six G burn for thirty minutes, and then drop down to cruising speed for the remainder of the trip. It should be a nice, comfortable journey for all of us."

As the timer counted down, Erik checked with Aurora to make sure all the crew not in the control room were safely strapped in to their crash couches. The couches were chairs that could pivot with the thrust of the ship, filled with a gel mixture that could harden when needed and be soft enough to absorb any sudden movements so that the fragile bodies of the crew were protected from harm. They were comfortable enough to spend a few hours in, but not comfortable enough that anyone would want to be stuck in them for too long.

Aurora started a verbal countdown for the final twenty seconds before acceleration, and then the ion engines flared to push the ship out and away from Earth and her moon. Erik was pushed back in his couch, and felt the gel harden around his body to provide more protection. A six G burn was the maximum he allowed without forcing everyone to stuff themselves into special high gravity suits that could increase tolerance to up to five times as much force, but it was enough to increase their speed quickly so that the resulting continuous one G burn would get them to the belt in a matter of months.

The rattles and intermittent shaking started immediately, and he closed his eyes to try to shut out the noise and worries it conjured up. Instead, he thought more about the note sent by Dex, and started to daydream about all the possible scenarios that could arise if he asked her out and she accepted. The pleasant thoughts occupied his mind better than expected, and he was surprised to hear the tone that signified the hard burn was complete. His eyes darted across the displays in front of him, gratified to see that his ship had survived the process once again.

When he left the control room a few hours later, he wandered the silent corridors knowing that aside from the pilot his crew was tucked into their bunks getting rest after a long day. His hand trailed along the cool steel bulkhead, feeling the steady thrum of the engines pushing the ship through space. As much as he had sometimes resented the ship when he was a teenager, he loved her now more than anything else. *Vagabond* was not only his home, but the only reminder he had left of his father.

He could still remember the first time he boarded the ship, eleven years old and already missing friends he was leaving behind in Iowa. He had sulked through the corridors as his father proudly pointed out fixes and enhancements that had been made to the freighter since using up most of his life savings to buy it. To the boy, it was a trash heap stinking of leaking coolant and rust that signified loneliness and shattered dreams. He never looked up from the ground long enough to see the joy and excitement shining in his father's eyes as they toured the ship.

"She may not look like much, son, but this ship is going to bring us our fortune." Edvald Frost had wrapped an arm around his young son. "Every credit of profit we make on our freight runs will be spent to improve her, too. Before you know it, the old girl will be one of the fastest ships in the system. This guild for freighters will make it easier to negotiate great rates on shipping contracts, and we're getting in at the beginning."

His father's dreams had never materialized, however, as the fledgling guild he joined faced stiff competition from ship captains that refused to give up their total freedom and took lower and lower rates to stay afloat. By the time all independent freighters belonged to the guild, the elder Frost's debts had mounted to a level he could not hope to pay off any time soon.

Entering his small but tidy cabin, Erik stripped off his jumpsuit and tossed it into the sanitizer drawer to be cleaned while he slept. His boots were left lying by the door, ready to be stepped into when he left the cabin. He crawled into his warm bunk, zipped himself in, and was asleep in moments.

Over the next few weeks, the crew settled in to the routines of traveling between far-flung colonies. Erik spent a portion of his day checking in with each person on the ship, lending a hand where needed to complete repairs and upkeep on the myriad systems that kept their home functioning smoothly. The camaraderie of the crew was evident in the way one of them could wordlessly know when to help out with a task, a byproduct of the many years spent together.

During the second week of the voyage, he worked with Tuya to strengthen welds on the supports of the catwalk running around the cargo bay. Though the job required concentration, they managed to trade a few friendly barbs and it reassured him that the frustration of the earlier argument was behind them. As they put the welding gear back into storage lockers, Erik's eyes were drawn to the dark container and his curiosity about what could be inside flared up.

"What could be in there?" he asked himself, not realizing he spoke the words aloud.

"Nothing but trouble," Tuya replied with a clenched jaw. He could see that she looked away from the pod, and tried to remember if he had ever seen her look in that direction as they worked on the catwalks above.

"You have experience with jobs like this one, don't you?"

Sighing wearily, she plopped down on a bench near the lockers and finally looked over at the container, hatred sparking in her eyes. "I've never seen one before in my life, and I had hoped to never do so." Erik watched her with interest, sensing she was considering whether to say more.

"I had a brother, Altan. He was five years older than me, and left home to join a guild ship when he turned eighteen. My parents tried to make him stay in Mongolia, tried to get him to join the Syndicate navy, but he was entranced with the romance of traveling the system in a freighter.

"He sent me messages all the time about whatever new thing he had seen or learned, and would talk with us over the video link when he had the chance." Tuya paused and smiled wistfully at the memories. "You should have seen how happy and excited he was about every little thing. I remember he spent an entire message talking about how complex docking maneuvers with an asteroid colony could be.

"By the time I was fifteen, I was dreaming of joining him on the ship as quickly as I was out of high school. He never got rich, but always sent some credits home after each voyage when he got his pay for the trip. My family was poor, so the money was always a huge boon and it made my parents so proud of him that he could help provide for us. I was working up the courage to tell them I was following in his footsteps, and planned to do so as soon as he returned from the trip he was on at that time."

Tuya swallowed a few times and wiped moisture from her eyes with one hand. Mouth tightening, she plowed ahead. "He had been especially excited about that trip, but he never gave more than vague hints about why it was different from any previous voyage out to the belt. The last message I received from him said only that he was close to a big payday and would send me all the credits I needed to buy gear and join his ship. He even hinted that one of his crewmates was talking of retiring when they returned to Luna, so that I'd have a spot to apply for.

"Seven months went by after that message, and we never heard from him. We asked the guild for any information they could give us, but no one that my parents spoke to could even say if the ship had reached its destination safely. My father finally scraped up every spare credit we had and made the trip to Luna so he could visit the Guild Hall in person. He sat in the hall for days, asking for any news they could give about my brother.

"On the fifteenth day, one of the guild reps approached him and told him they had just received reports that debris from my brother's ship had been found. The ship had been obliterated, and the only thing they ever recovered aside from small bits of hull plating was the transponder. Because it was in the belt, the assumption was that they had collided with an asteroid. Perhaps the engines had issues and sent them off course, perhaps the rock had left its projected course and wasn't picked up by the AI soon enough, perhaps it was just a dumb accident."

Erik reached across and placed a hand on her shoulder. "I am so sorry, Tuya. I know how hard it is to lose a family member, and how much harder it is to never know why or how." After a moment, the timing of the events locked into place in his head. "Wait .... your brother was on the *Telemachus*? My dad knew the captain of that ship. He took it hard when we heard the news. It was the first guild ship to be lost."

"That wasn't the end of it, though," she said, eyes going to the dark container across the bay again. "When I turned eighteen, I was working in the dockyards on Luna. I had been trying to find a berth on a ship unsuccessfully, and took a job hauling and storing cargo to get by. I celebrated my birthday with a few friends and got back to my room late in the evening to find a message waiting, marked urgent. It was from my brother." Tuya turned shining eyes on her captain, reliving the disbelief and confusion experienced when she saw the message.

"At first I thought it had to be some kind of sick joke, but as soon as I started reading it I knew the message was really from Altan. It was something he had typed up and stored on a private server days before his last message to us years before, and he had coded in a rule that sent it to me on my eighteenth birthday if he didn't delete it. I won't share everything that was in the message, but I can tell you that I deleted it and removed any trace of it once I finished reading. The words were seared in my memory, and I didn't want anyone to ever find it."

Tuya hesitated and took a deep breath, as if steeling herself to say the words. Erik could see that this message was a burden she had been carrying for a long time, and he wished he could help relieve her of it.

"Altan told me that his captain had accepted a special job from the guild, something that was going to make them all rich. His share from that one job was supposed to be as much as he'd made on all the previous trips. He didn't say who the job was for, but he described the cargo container very well." She grimaced and raised a shaking hand to point at the strange container. "It was just like that one, Frost. Right down to the console that won't let anyone access it and the dark blue color. Until I saw this thing in our bay, I had no idea what kind of job they might have gotten involved in, but I know it's the reason that ship was destroyed and my brother is dead."

They both stared wordlessly at the oddly shaped container for long moments, lost in unpleasant thoughts. Erik wished he had asked for more details about the job before accepting it, knowing his greed had led him to act without caution. He had skimmed through his father's old ship logs trying to find any notes or details on the times he made trips to the black sites, but had found nothing. He resolved to send a message to Dex as soon as he got back to his cabin to see if she could provide more information or give him dates from those old contracts.

He was shaken from his reverie when the cargo specialist spoke again. "I'd appreciate it if you kept all of this between us, Frost. I don't like to talk about my family, and I've never told anyone about how we lost my brother before."

"I promise that no one will hear about it from me," Erik promised. "I would never have taken the job if I had known any of this. You know that, right?"

She smiled faintly at her captain, and nodded. "You're a good man, Frost. I don't blame you for any of this. I know that at least a part of you took the job with the thought of improving all our lives."

"The money was far too good to pass up," he said with chagrin. "It's possible something unrelated did happen to the *Telemachus*. When we heard about it, my dad and the crew hashed out all kinds of theories about what caused the ship to be destroyed."

"Yeah, I spent a few years doing the same thing. I'd be convinced it was an errant asteroid for a few days, and then be sure it was a reactor meltdown from shoddy maintenance or something. We both know how watchful pilots and AIs are for the asteroid to be unlikely, and we know these ships are too well cared for to allow a meltdown. The odds are far too low for either to explain it."

"No matter how low the odds, it has to happen to someone at some point. A few years into my stint on a Coalition frigate, our ship got hit by a micro meteor storm that none of the sensors had picked up. Thousands of tiny projectiles no larger than my thumbnail, and most barely larger than a grain of sand, hammering against the hull for less than a minute. The odds of those particles getting through the thick hull plating are tiny, and yet half a dozen made it through. We lost two people to that storm, and spent a week repairing all the damage."

"I know, stranger things have been known to happen. You just never expect anything like that to happen to someone you know and love. I miss him so much."

He wrapped an arm around her. Shaking shoulders told him she was crying as the old feelings overwhelmed her. After a while, Tuya wiped a hand across her eyes and gave a final sniff. She stood and finished stuffing gear in the storage locker, and turned to leave the cargo bay. Over her shoulder, she quietly said "Thanks for listening, captain. I hadn't realized how much I'd bottled up."

Erik remained on the bench for a few minutes after she left, running through dozens of scenarios in his head to explain the lost ship. None of them seemed to call out as the obvious answer, and yet all of them were somewhat likely to have happened. He finally pushed aside his new concerns, and followed the cargo specialist from the bay. It was time to send some messages and try to get answers to questions he should have asked in the beginning.

A week later, Erik was still in the dark about the black site delivery. Dex had finally responded with the barest amount of information he'd ever received for a shipping contract. The message merely detailed who the delivery was for, highlighted the need for security and confidentiality, and listed the exorbitant payment due once the job was completed.

Sorry, she wrote at the bottom of the message. *This is all the data that we're allowed to see. A strongly encrypted data packet was sent to your AI when you accepted the contract, but I know it included commands and directives that prevent the information from being shared. Those commands also wipe the entire packet from the AI memory cores when the contract is fulfilled.*

Erik had tried to talk to Aurora about the container, but the AI would not even confirm that a data packet with information about the job had been received. He had discussed the issue with Isaac, and the ship's technician tried poking around in the AI's codes and subroutines.

"Sorry, captain," he reported hours later. "I've dug through Aurora's code as much as I can, but I'm not finding anything that looks out of the ordinary. Her memory cores are running at the usual levels, but those can fluctuate by hundreds of terabytes on a day-to-day basis depending on what operations she is currently running."

"What about data coming into the ship's network while we were in the dock?"

"Nothing there, either," Isaac said regretfully. "We were all sending and receiving messages, I was pulling in software updates from Luna's servers, and the ship was also pulling in new entertainment packages for the rec room. There was too much data flowing in and out."

The technician paused in thought for a few moments, and then mused, "If I was going to send a data packet that was this important and didn't want it found, I'd include a command that scrubbed the records so it wouldn't be found if anyone looked."

"Aurora could do that? Hide the data so well that even you couldn't see a trace of it?"

Isaac grinned proudly and patted the console in front of him with pride. "My girl is smarter than your average AI, captain. I don't scrub the memory banks every few months like other techs do, so she's gained more intelligence with all the knowledge allowed to build up in her cores."

Erik pinched the bridge of his nose in frustration. "It might be time to consider reining her in a little, Isaac. I don't know that I like having an AI that can be running programs and making decisions that affect all of us without leaving any kind of trace."

The tech looked crestfallen at the thought, but nodded. "I'll make sure to do a memory purge the next time we're in dock. But just a light one," he added forcefully. "I'm not going to strip all personality and originality from my girl."

"This black site job is supposed to be so locked down that Aurora will be in charge of the ship's navigation for the entire trip there and back from Interamnia. Do you think she's capable of handling that, Isaac?"

"Without a doubt, captain! The first moon lander over a hundred years ago ran on computers so primitive they were little more than simple calculators, and yet that landing was successful with only minimal human interaction. Our modern AIs, even the cheap versions running no more than a single home network, are infinitely more capable. Aurora can navigate the ship through almost any environment and safely dock or land at our destination. The Syndicate even considered ships that were entirely controlled by AI, without any human crew at all, for their exploration beyond the asteroid belt. The only reason the Executive Committee overruled the idea was because of the strong bias against AI without a controlling human influence."

"That's good to know," Eric said with a grateful sigh. "I don't think that I'd be comfortable flying in a ship piloted by the AI all the time, but it's good to know we can trust her for a short duration. It's supposed to only be several weeks for the total trip, a month at the most."

Isaac grinned mischievously and looked at the open door of the tech hub that was across the hall from the control room. "Honestly, I don't know why we keep John around at all, except to push buttons."

"I heard that!" the pilot called out. "Be happy I don't push the button to eject your ass from the nearest airlock."

The technician snickered softly, and waved as Erik left the room. *Only a few more months and this cargo will be delivered,* he reminded himself, promising to never accept a job like this again.

THREE

A little more than halfway through the curving voyage across the system to rendezvous with Interamnia, Erik was dragged from his slumber as his body was thrown to the side within the cocoon of his bed. Even within the protective wrapping, he could feel the increased weight of a high G burn. After a few seconds, the force lessened and he rolled into an uncomfortable position. The bedding had been tangled around him, and he fought to get his hand through the twists of material to reach the zipper that kept him inside the tight confines.

Extracting himself with fumbling fingers, Erik pivoted and sat up. After stretching his arms and legs for a moment, he moved across the small cabin to pull on some clothes and step into his boots. Stumbling into the corridor, he hurried to the reactor room. He was thankful to see the radiation levels in the green as he opened the hatch, and jogged past the nuclear reactor and into the engine room at the rear of the ship. The engineer was stuffed into an open wall panel, feet jerking rhythmically as he hastily worked on something unseen.

"Fynn, what's going on?"

"The ion thrusters have gone crazy," a muffled voice replied. "The damn things keep firing off with no…"

The voice was cut off with a yelp as the ship jumped forward under sudden thrust, throwing Erik against the bulkhead. White flashed before his eyes as his head made contact with the unyielding wall. The force of the acceleration held him tightly to the bulkhead as he struggled to breathe against what felt like bands of iron around his lungs. Suddenly, with as little warning as they flared up, the engines died down and the G forces were lifted from his body.

Ears ringing and a trickle of blood beginning to obscure the vision in one eye, Erik pulled himself along the bulkhead toward the open panel. He could hear the engineer moaning in pain as he got closer, and kneeled down to peer into the space so he could assess the situation.

"How are you doing in there, Fynn?"

Groaning and wriggling to try to extract himself from the tight space, Jesperson cursed the engines in disgust. "I think my wrist is broken, captain. That thrust was much stronger than the previous ones, and I wasn't in a good position to handle it."

Erik helped pull the engineer from the confines of the access panel, gingerly taking hold of the man's right arm and looking at a wrist already turning an ominous purple shade. "Aurora, alert Dr. Murphy that she is needed in Engineering."

"Belay that," Fynn called out immediately, pulling his arm away and holding it tight against his chest as he sat on the floor near the panel. "Let the crew know we're working on the issue and they should strap into a crash couch to be safe." He took short breaths, visibly fighting the pain in his wrist. "We can't let anyone else move around, captain, until we get the engines repaired. It's just risking more injuries, and probably worse ones at that."

"You're right," Erik conceded, turning to look over the engine room but not seeing anything out of the ordinary. "When did the malfunction begin?"

"That was the third instance, and they seem to be happening every ten to fifteen minutes so far. The first one was minimal, but I happened to be checking a few things in the reactor room when it happened. If I'd been in my bunk like the rest of you, we might not have known anything was amiss until this last incident. They are getting stronger, and I don't know how much more we can take."

While the engineer was talking, Erik had grabbed the first aid kit nearby and was working to put a makeshift splint on Jesperson's wrist, then passed the man a few painkillers to help ease the discomfort. He also wiped the blood away from the cut on his own forehead and slapped a bandage over it to prevent more bleeding from hindering his vision. That task completed, he put the kit away and helped the engineer to his feet. "Let me be your hands, just tell me what I need to do."

"I'll keep checking the cables and connections here, since I was almost done with them." He pointed to the other side of the large room, motioning toward the bulkhead farthest from the reactor room. "Go over to panel 3A71 and check in there. You've worked with me enough to know what you're looking for."

Erik rushed across the room, deftly unlocked the panel and set it aside. The uncovered opening was a few feet up from the deck and only eighteen inches tall, making it a tight fit as he bent and leaned into the portal. Conduits of varying sizes snaked through the space behind the bulkhead, dozens of them with very little clearance between them. Years of experience working on the ship helped him to quickly differentiate which conduits belonged to which system on the ship; blue conduits contained wiring for the computer systems, green denoted wiring that connected the command room to everything across the ship, and so on. The red conduits contained wiring and tubing for the engines and reactor room, so he sorted quickly through the jumble to find those and retracted sections to check integrity of the cabling within, making sure to snap the sections back together when he was done.

After verifying the wiring in the panel was good, he replaced the cover and moved a few feet along to the next one. He could feel the pressure of an invisible timer counting down in his head as he fumbled through the conduits to check them. Find the red conduit, retract cover, check the wires, close cover, move to next red conduit. He knew that he should be happy to see the contents of the myriad conduits so well maintained and undamaged, but his frustration grew each time he failed to find a problem that could be causing the engine malfunctions. He was checking wiring in the fourth panel, sweat dripping down his face and back, when Fynn called out to him.

"Captain, if the pattern holds the engines are going to fire at any moment. We need to get strapped in."

Both men quickly closed the panels they were checking, and hurried across to the three crash couches around the central consoles, where an engineering crew could monitor ship functions. Fynn strapped in at his usual couch at the central console while Erik took the couch to his left. After they were both secure, the engineer reached out with his good hand and clumsily tapped at the console to bring up displays.

"I had Aurora start timing the malfunctions after the second instance. We're coming up on the same mark where the thrusters kicked in the third time."

"If the malfunction is happening on a regular cycle, does that help you narrow down what the problem could be?"

The engineer considered that while tapping through several screens, and finally shrugged. "I wish it did, but I can't think of any particular system or program that would misfire so regularly. I do have several diagnostics running this time, though, so hopefully if the thrusters fire again we'll get some data to help track down the root cause."

Erik tapped the console in front of him to bring it to life, and keyed in commands to check the status of the crew. The others were safely ensconced in their crash couches, and it looked like John had gone to control in case he was needed. He was pulling up the hull integrity statistics when the ion engines flared up again, pushing him back against the gel padding without warning.

Alerts began to blare as the roar of the engines grew into a deafening cacophony around the two men. Erik saw a message pop up on the console in front of him, warning that the ship was surpassing the six G threshold that he and his father had always followed as a safe limit. The number continued to climb, as did the pressure on his body as the forces increased. When the acceleration surpassed ten G's, he felt as if he could not draw in a breath and the force against his body was so strong he could barely move at all.

The alert noises grew louder and more insistent, rivaling the noise of the engines and the rattling of the ship as it experienced forces that it had not seen in more than a decade. Just as blackness was creeping into his vision and he felt on the verge of passing out, the engine thrust plummeted to normal cruising levels and he was almost thrown forward with the release of force.

Fynn coughed weakly next to him, wheezing breaths audible over the now humming engines. Erik quickly unstrapped himself and hurried over to the engineer's crash couch. A trickle of blood was trailing from the corner of the man's mouth, and his face was a mask of pain.

"I think a few ribs cracked, and might have punctured a lung," Fynn croaked out, obviously struggling with each breath. He winced through a short chuckle. "It's not turning out to be my day at all."

"Aurora, let Dr. Murphy know I'm bringing Fynn to the med bay." He unstrapped Fynn, and helped the man stand and begin a shuffling walk through the reactor room.

"The diagnostics picked up on something just before that last burn," the engineer gasped out between steps. "It looks like the malfunction is consistent, too, so you should be able to anticipate the next one."

"Don't worry about any of that right now," Erik told him as he saw Sally step into the corridor ahead of them. "I'll get back to the engine room as soon as you're being looked at, and dig into things again." The doctor hurried to help him support the engineer as they entered the med bay. "Anyone else hurt during that last burn?"

"Thankfully, no," Sally Murphy told him. "You have all of our thanks for upgrading the crash couches a few years ago. Those old models would have failed for sure at the extreme forces we just experienced, and I don't want to think how bad things would have been then."

Once Fynn was safely ensconced in a diagnostic chair that also functioned as a crash couch, the captain hurried from the room. "Take care of him, doc," he called as he left. He paused in the reactor room long enough to turn on the ship's intercom. "Everyone get into your high G suits immediately. If we can't fix the problem before the next malfunction, it's going to be a rough one. Tuya, John, meet me in the engine room as soon as you're suited up."

Erik released the comms button and pulled one of the high G suits from a locker. It wasn't a perfect fit, but he didn't want to waste time going back to his cabin for the custom-fitted suit there. As he reached the main console, he saw a timer counting down in the upper left corner. Undoubtedly, that was when the next expected malfunction would occur.

He spoke urgently, eyes looking up. "Aurora, do an audible count when that timer hits thirty seconds, and make sure everyone gets strapped in. In the meantime, go through the diagnostics Fynn has running and see what you can find. Nothing is jumping out at me here, but he saw something that might explain the problem."

"I am working on it now, captain," the gentle feminine voice reassured him.

Tuya arrived seconds later, with John not far behind her. Erik pulled up a schematic of the room and pointed out the access panels that had not been checked for faulty or loose wiring yet. The two crew members set to work on checking conduits while he started running a detailed program that would shoot a signal through each wire individually looking for any faults. Concurrently, the diagnostic would run a quality control check on the programs that told the engines what to do and when to do it. Erik was sure his engineer had already checked these things, but he had to be sure before moving down the list of troubleshooting.

The audible countdown began as they worked, and Erik ordered everyone to get strapped in. As soon as Aurora announced the last second, the engines burst into life once more. Even through the protective suits, he could feel the intense pressure of the burn as it reached fourteen G's before fading back to cruising speed. The three of them jumped from the couches as quickly as possible to get back to trying to find the cause.

"Captain," Sally called over the intercom, breaking his concentration. "I have Fynn sedated while the nanobots are knitting his bones back together, but before he went out he said I should tell you to look at point seven. I hope you know what he meant by that."

Erik felt a vague memory at the words, and John roared in laughter from inside the panel he was checking. Extracting himself, the pilot smiled over at his captain with a hopeful expression.

"It's probably been too long, captain, but don't you remember your lessons when Fynn was teaching you how the ship worked?"

He grunted as the memories returned of the many weeks spent pouring over the engines and programs that controlled them when he was a teenager. "Oh yeah, he had that list of the most important things to remember when working on his delicate engines."

"Fynn's Twelve Points of Important Knowledge, he calls them," John said, grinning at the memory. "And if my memory is good, point seven was..."

"Never forget the tertiary power coupling," both men pronounced together as Tuya looked on with a raised eyebrow. Fynn had always been adamant that one layer of redundancy was not enough for safety, and insisted on putting in a second backup for all of his systems. It was an extra expense that very few ships took on, but it had saved the *Vagabond* from serious troubles a few times over the years.

They hurried over to the ceiling access panel where the power couplings connected to the main engine power input, Erik jumping up to release the panel while John pulled a small ladder from a nearby locker.

Erik climbed the ladder as Aurora started the next verbal countdown warning that another malfunction was expected within thirty seconds. "Get in the couches," he ordered John and Tuya, wanting to know they were safe in case this was not the fix.

"You need to get strapped in yourself, Frost." Tuya said urgently as she settled into the gel cushioning and started to connect the restraints.

Ignoring her, he reached up to push aside the thick cables of the main and secondary power lines, and began to smell the carbon from a burnt coupler. The tertiary coupling was singed and melted in some parts, with the cable to either side of it scored black. It was a small miracle that whatever had caused the damage had not spread to the tightly packed cabling around it or to the engine itself.

"Five," the soft voice of the AI said.

He grabbed both sides of the metal coupling collar, and twisted with all his strength. At first, it seemed that the damage was too great to allow the parts to turn.

"Four."

He felt his grip beginning to slip on the smooth metal.

"Three."

With a jerk, the collar began to rotate.

"Two."

The two cables, now separated, hung loosely with the damaged couple tapping against the bulkhead.

"One."

Erik jumped down from the ladder and ran to the empty crash couch, connecting the restraints in a silence broken only by a soft hum of the ion thrusters working at normal capacity. Tense minutes followed as the three crewmates waited with bated breath for another wild thrust. As time ticked by without a malfunction, they began to relax and hope that the damaged power coupler truly was the cause of the problems.

Erik waited through another full countdown before breathing a deep sigh of relief and giving the all clear for everyone to leave the crash couches. He asked them to keep the high G suits on until they could be absolutely sure the issues would not return. He, John, and Tuya began a series of intensive diagnostic tests and continued checking all the wiring to rule out any problems there. Once all the diagnostics passed successfully, Tuya set to work replacing the tertiary power cables that had been damaged, while John dug through storage closets to find a replacement coupler.

Several hours after being woken from his short sleep, Erik surveyed the fixes to the damaged parts and nodded with satisfaction. "It looks like we got that fixed just in time."

"Definitely," Tuya said, motioning at the central console. "I looked over Fynn's notes about the force of the thrusts, and if the engines fired another time on the same sliding scale we would have been looking at more than twenty three G's of thrust, the maximum power for our engines."

John winced at the thought of so much pressure on their fragile human bodies. "Any one of us could have stroked out with that much sustained force. I've experienced as much before in emergency situations, but that was always short bursts of a second or two."

"I heard horror stories about long maneuvers with almost as much acceleration when I was on a frigate," Erik told them, struggling to get out of the high gravity suit now that the danger was past. "When the Coalition and Syndicate were actively fighting each other a few decades back, it was apparently a common occurrence when two of their ships engaged in battle. The lieutenant I served under was a grizzled old veteran, and he'd been through a couple of firefights himself. He said the crew was forced to live in the compression suits, and still the injury lists after each engagement were filled with people who suffered broken bones or burst blood vessels in a hard burn."

The three finished putting the engine room in order, and then went their separate ways. Tuya headed to the cargo bay to check the pod and containers, John retreated to his pilot's station in the control room to run checks on how far the engine bursts might have pushed them off course, and Erik checked in on the engineer in the med bay. Learning from Sally that the nanobots were still at work making repairs to the broken bones and punctured lung, he finally returned to his cabin, wearily undressing and crawling back into his bunk. With the adrenaline wearing off, he felt as if he had just done twenty miles on the rec room spinner. Sleep claimed him almost as soon as he closed his eyes.

Four days after the excitement of the malfunctioning engines, Fynn woke from sedated slumber to find his young captain sitting at the bedside. The clunky nanobots had finally completed the repairs to his body earlier in the day as well as they could, and the doctor had extracted the small amount of black sludge that remained from the expended devices. The remnants were stored away to be sold at a future port for recycling purposes; the metals and plastics that the nanobots were created from could be melted down and reused to make more of the medical marvels. That small income helped offset by a small margin the purchase of an expensive replacement set of nanobots.

"Was it Seven?" the engineer asked in a croaking voice.

"Never forget the tertiary power couple," Erik said with a smile. "You were right as always, old friend."

The engineer gave a wan smile and licked dry lips. "I'm glad you remembered my lessons. I seem to recall a moody young man that spent more time moping and playing games on his tablet than paying attention to what I said."

Erik poured some water into a cup and helped Fynn take a few sips. He could see that the older man was still in a lot of pain from the mostly repaired bones and lung. "I'll confess that John had to help jog my memory, but I do remember most of the things you taught me back then. I wish I'd paid more attention, though, and we could have fixed the problem before you got injured so badly. It looks like the coupling overheated at some point, and got hot enough to partially melt the metal collar and the connected cables."

Fynn groaned and raised a shaky hand to rap himself on the forehead. "I've been meaning to check on the power couplings for weeks, but something else always came up that seemed more important."

"It's okay, Fynn, there are a lot of things to keep your eye on in this old ship. I should have spent more time helping out in the engine room, rather than sitting in control watching all of you work."

"That's the captain's job," the engineer protested. "It may be a long count of years since I worked on another ship, but you and your father before you have always pitched in and done more hands-on work than any other captain I've known. Most treat it as a right, to be able to sit in that big chair and dictate what's done instead of doing it themselves."

Erik snorted in agreement, thinking of the captains he served under during his time in the Coalition navy. Other freighter captains were more willing to get their hands dirty keeping their ships functional, but he knew that most would only do so in emergency situations or if a member of their crew was incapacitated for one reason or another.

"Most ships also run a bit of a larger crew," he said. "I only know three other captains that have the same number of crew or fewer, and they have smaller ships than the *Vagabond*."

"Less complicated systems, too," Fynn agreed. "You're stuck with an old tinkerer for an engineer, who won't stop adding on to the basic engine setup."

"And a technician obsessed with turning our ship into the system's most intelligent AI." Erik laughed loudly and then looked upwards. "Isn't that right, Aurora?"

"My intelligence levels are well above standard for AI systems," the soft voice of the ship's computer replied evenly. "I surpassed Luna's level several months ago, but there are still seven AIs on Earth that score marginally higher on the IQ tests."

"Humble, too," Fynn said under his breath, and the men shared a laugh.

Erik gave the man a friendly pat on the arm, and then made his exit so Fynn could get rest. It would be another day or two before Sally let him out of the med bay to resume his duties, and Erik planned to make sure his engineer had no reason to regret being away from his engines for so long.

FOUR

The remainder of the voyage passed smoothly for the *Vagabond* and her crew. The malfunctioning engines had only caused minor course corrections, and in the end they approached the mining colony on Interamnia a few days ahead of schedule.

Navigating through the asteroid belt was always a tense time for Erik and his pilot. Despite the vast distances between the multitude of rocks orbiting the sun, occasional collisions caused deviations in projected paths and John had to keep a vigilant eye on the sensors. Aurora alerted them of deviations almost immediately, but there were rare instances where the pilot's experience let him see a problem developing before the sensors and AI picked up on it.

As the dense asteroid grew larger on the holographic display that projected the view from the front of the ship, Erik sent a standard message to the colony with his ship information, cargo they were delivering, and a list of supplies they would like to purchase if available. The asteroid's sensor station had picked up the ship's transponder signal well before that point, but there was a decorum involved with space travel that all ships followed. It had been almost a decade since the Coalition and Syndicate fleets last swept the belt to clear out a growing pirate menace, but the habits built up during the tense period of random attacks had survived and been strengthened in the years since.

John announced the braking burn a few hours out from the colony, and masterfully slowed the ship so that they achieved docking speed mere minutes before reaching the rapidly spinning asteroid. With Aurora's help, he maneuvered the ship toward the tunnel bored into the asteroid in the earliest days of the colony, and entered with only a few dozen meters to spare on all sides; larger ships had to land on the asteroid itself, and pay a fee to use the miners' small cargo shuttle.

Small lights were set at regular intervals throughout the long tunnel, highlighting rough-hewn rock that was many times denser and stronger than that quarried on Earth. Random glinting or darker spots denoted pockets of mostly iron and iridium, with small amounts of tungsten, cobalt and aluminum found sprinkled through the asteroid. The miners had pulled up miniscule amounts of other ores, but the primary export to Luna and Earth was iridium. The ore was highly prized for its many medical, industrial and scientific uses, as well as being used in many electronic devices. The *Vagabond* itself contained a hefty amount of iridium in its infrastructure.

The tunnel flared out half a kilometer in to provide enough space for a docking platform, backed by a solid wall of thick steel that contained the atmosphere within the inhabited space. The steel was smelted from the iron dug out of the asteroid and sifted from the more valuable ores that were shipped back to Earth.

It had taken many years for the space to be hollowed out and pressurized, during which the early colonists had lived in small shelters built from hard plastic walls that were lighter than steel and cheaper to ship out so far into the system. From that early beginning of a handful of hardy souls, the colony had become home for a growing population that was counted in the hundreds.

John set the ship down gently on the landing pad, and tapped in a few commands on his console to request connection to the firm but flexible tube that would attach the ship to the colony. They watched as a door retracted and the tube extended out from the wall to connect with one of the *Vagabond's* airlocks. An audible thunk could be heard throughout the ship as the collar attached to the ship with an airtight seal, and a chime sounded in the control room to confirm.

Erik keyed the comms and announced, "Ladies and gentlemen, we have arrived at our destination. Secure the ship, gather your shopping lists, and prepare for a few days of relaxation." He smiled as a muffled cheer could be heard from the scattered crew, and tapped a few buttons to open a video link with the Interamnia control center. Within seconds, the display in front of him was replaced with the image of a stern-faced woman with short gray hair. "Captain Frost of the freighter *Vagabond*, requesting permission to enter the colony."

The woman on the display nodded perfunctorily, and motioned to someone outside of his view. "Request approved, captain. Welcome back to Interamnia. Our dock foreman is in contact with your cargo specialist and making arrangements to extract the cargo pod and containers you have brought for us. Payment has been authorized to be processed as soon as the deliveries are complete."

"Excellent news, control. A pleasure dealing with you, as always,"

"Your sentiment is shared, captain." One side of the woman's mouth moved upwards in a quick smile. "Tell Fynn I expect him to meet me at the Silver Sunrise tonight. No excuses."

Erik chuckled. Agatha Crisp, the head of Interamnia's small government, had been openly courting the old engineer since before Erik took over the captain's chair. Jesperson proclaimed that he had no interest in romantic entanglements, but the other members of the crew had noticed that he always returned from visits with the woman in a much better mood and that he would smile spontaneously for weeks after leaving the asteroid. "I'll personally deliver him, ma'am." Erik threw a mock salute as the video link was closed.

"Silver Sunrise, huh?" John spoke up from his station where he had been eavesdropping. "Best bar on the rock, so Agatha's pulling out all the stops to try and get at Fynn's crusty old heart."

Once the rest of the crew left the ship to complete minor restocking and sample the local entertainments, Erik entered the airlock and engaged the security locks. He had no reason to expect an interloper, but caution was ingrained in his nature. Aurora would contact him via his tablet should anyone try to tamper with the locks or enter the ship without inputting one of the crew's codes.

Exiting the airlock on the opposite side of the docking tube, he breathed in the smell of Interamnia. It was a mixture of sweat from decades of hard-working miners, a bit of moist earth from the hydroponics platforms that grew food for the citizens, and a touch of the hot metallic scent that generations of astronauts and space farers had described as the smell of the dark vacuum. The central space of the colony was a large quarried-out cavern, several hundred meters in both directions with a height that varied from ten meters at the edges to three times as much in the middle. Two roads split the cavern in either direction, bisecting at a central square surrounded by the only planned buildings erected soon after the cavern was excavated. All the buildings and pathways that grew up around them were organic additions added as dictated by need and whim.

Just to the left of the entry airlock was the warehouse that stored pods and containers that were arriving or waiting to be shipped out on the next available freighter. The cargo bay of his ship would be depressurized and the large double doors at the nose of the ship would swing open horizontally so that the colony cargo handlers could use computer-controlled equipment around the docking platform to transfer the cargo from the ship and into a portion of the warehouse that could be depressurized in the same way until everything was moved inside. Erik could see Tuya just inside the wide open doors chatting with a few of the cargo handlers as they prepared to unload the shipment from *Vagabond*. He knew that she would keep a careful eye on the operators and guided machinery, ensuring that no damage was done to the ship or other cargo.

The artificial spin of the asteroid provided enough gravity to make the inhabitants comfortable, which Erik appreciated as he walked down the central pathway. He passed groups of colonists hard at work or enjoying leisure time. He returned friendly waves, and was stopped once by an amiable old man who asked for any news the captain had to share that might not have come in on the newsfeeds.

Not far from the square, he entered a narrow two level building with a storefront on the bottom and living quarters above. Inside, the guild representative for Interamnia was sitting behind a desk quickly typing up reports and checking various screens on his console. The middle aged man looked up when he realized he was no longer alone, and smiled in greeting.

"Hello, Captain Frost. A little earlier than I expected to see you."

Erik leaned forward to shake hands with the representative, and took a seat in front of the gray plastic desk. "We had a few issues with the ion engines on the way in, with a net result of a bit more speed than expected."

"Issues that have happy resolutions are the best kind to have," the representative said, turning to peruse the data scrolling across a display until he found what he needed.

"I see you have two contracts that are being offloaded here, with one more for your next stop. Looks like the security on it is above my access level. Seems important," the man said without sounding as if he was curious about the details in the slightest.

"It pays well, but I'll be happy to get that job completed and off my ship."

"Yes, I've seen a number of captains come through here over the years with similar contracts. It's amazing to me how few of them come through again after that, but I guess they found better things to do with their credits." The rep clapped his hands as if dismissing the subject, and rubbed them together vigorously. "Let's see if we have anything that you can take off my hands while you're here."

"I'm planning to return to Luna after this last job, but I can take some detours if the pay is worth it."

Erik spent most of an hour in the guild office, looking through available jobs on Interamnia and those listed for other colonies near the return path to Luna. He haggled with the representative mercilessly, both of them enjoying the experience, and finally took on a load of two cargo pods of ore that were in the nearby warehouse. Delivery to Luna would cover running costs of the return trip, and leave some credits to line the crew's pockets as well.

He left the guild outpost whistling a happy tune and continued on to the central square. The air was cooler than average as a result of cheap insulation layers installed between the steel walls and the open rock surfaces that surrounded the colony's inhabited spaces, so the citizens on the streets or relaxing in the square wore heavy clothing to keep in their body heat. Children running around the legs of their parents and other adults kept themselves warm enough to work up a sweat and shed their outer layers as soon as they felt they could get away with it. Nonetheless, it was a pleasant place to live and the colony accepted a dozen or so new citizens from around the system every year.

Erik thought back over the changes he had seen since his first stops on the asteroid when he was not much older than the children playing along the path. In those early days, the colony had consisted of a few dozen rough miners and a few of their wives. There had been plastic-shelled habitats tucked into a small crater on the surface of Interamnia, thick enough to protect those inside from the radiation and cold of space.

By the time he was fifteen, the miners had been joined by a group of scientists eager to examine all the materials coming out of the shaft being dug deep into the rock surface. There were nearly sixty colonists in total by then, filling the space within the temporary habitats in the crater. The smell of old plastic could still make Erik think of days spent in those sparse rooms as his father negotiated contracts to transport ores and spoils back to Luna. It had been less than a year before the caverns were completed and the colonists moved into the newly pressurized space.

On his first trip as captain of the *Vagabond*, he found a thriving colony that was close to filling the excavated interior of the asteroid. The hydroponics had been expanded to provide for most of the nutritional needs of the inhabitants, and the people living in the small homes seemed to be happy with the freedom of life on an independent colony. More than three hundred people called Interamnia home by then. Most were drawn by the fantasy of striking it rich with mining or by the freedom of living in the colonies, no longer under Coalition or Syndicate rule.

Entering the colonial administration building felt like a step back in time. This was the first permanent building constructed on the asteroid, and in the tradition of governments going back thousands of years very few credits were spent on upgrades to the space. The administration center had been built for function and efficiency that did not require fancy furnishings or the most up-to-date materials. As a consequence, the building felt close and dark after the wide open square and looked much like old pictures Erik's father used to show him of the older man's boyhood on Earth.

He checked in with the small guard station by the door, and made his way up a flight of stairs to the offices on the second level. His first stop was to authorize payment for docking fees and tariffs used to pay the small taxes levied on the colonies by the Coalition. Those taxes were nominal and largely ceremonial now that the colonies governed themselves and survived off the sale of mined ores to the home world. The Earth-based government still provided a modicum of security by sending a frigate through the trade routes on rare occasions.

Next, Erik made his way into the main hub of the building, a large room that was lined with consoles around the edges and dominated by a central platform housing a semicircular desk. He nodded at the governor on the platform, and navigated through the room to chat with the dock master and get approval to keep *Vagabond* on the platform for a few days. He could have performed all of these tasks via video link, but he had learned from his father that it was important to communicate in person whenever possible to reinforce connections.

Leaving the administration building, he continued through the colony towards the far side of the cavern from the docking platforms. The buildings were soon replaced by the open-air platforms that were used as hydroponic fields, often containing five or six platforms placed in a column with the ability to slide up and down the side supports to allow access. At the moment the platforms were all evenly spaced with a few feet between them. The soft humming of the pumps that kept water flowing throughout the column and reclaimed any moisture that seeped to the bottom of each platform always made him feel hungry with the memory of the taste of the crisp vegetables that were grown.

There were sheds set farther back from the road that contained deeper indoor platforms. Soybeans were the biggest crop grown in those, for their many uses aside from feeding colonists, along with a small quantity of fruits that were as highly priced as they were desired.

Beyond the hydroponics was a long, low building that served as the scientific hub on the asteroid. The botanists in charge of the hydroponics fields were based there, along with geologists and chemists who examined the materials pulled from the rock by the miners. As the colony continued to grow past its small early population, a handful of other sciences were represented.

Erik made his way through a maze of hallways that often took sudden turns to go around spaces that had been expanded for larger work areas, and found the man he was looking for stuffed into a dark old corner of the building. The researcher was hunched over his workbench, an array of parts scattered before him, and the sleeves of his white coat pushed up beyond the elbows to keep them clear of the oil and grease that liberally covered his hands.

"I hope that wasn't something important," Erik said with a grin.

"Just one of the busted generator assemblies. I'm going to get it fixed, but I had a few ideas for improving the function and I wanted to see if they might be viable." The researcher kept tinkering for a minute before looking up. On seeing the captain his face broke out in a smile and he started to reach out a hand before remembering the residues and retracting it. "Erik! It's good to see you again."

"And a surprise, apparently, despite the message I sent you when we left Luna." Erik leaned on a clear space of the workbench, grinning at how absent-minded his friend could be.

"Yes, I did get your message. I was working on an upgrade to the hydroponic water flow system at the time, and that seems like only a few weeks ago."

"Only off by several months."

"Ah well, the work is the important thing. Time is nothing more than an annoyance." The man had already turned back to the parts before him, deftly plucking up the bit he had been looking for and examining it. Placing it into the housing of the generator, he soon connected it to the structure.

Erik knew he had to keep the researcher's attention, or he would get lost in his work again and forget about the visitor. "Robert, you said you wanted to see me the next time I came through. You had some important components or something you needed me to look for?"

"Oh, yes!" The man jumped from his stool, grabbing a stained cloth to wipe his hands. They crossed the lab to a heavy steel door. He keyed in a code to disengage the lock, and then waved Erik forward to see the blueprints tacked up to the wall of a room no larger than a closet. "I had the most outrageous idea one morning in the shower, and I've been working on it every chance I get between other projects."

The researcher almost seemed to purr with satisfaction as he ran his hands over the pages on the wall. "Fusion reactors have been the holy grail of energy production for decades. Of course, they have been built in the past, but never able to produce energy on a large scale. At first, the technology wasn't advanced enough, and then the early reactors proved unreliable and not as profitable as the already operating fission reactors. I started thinking about the processes used in those fusion reactors, though, and had an epiphany. I could reroute the flow of hydrogen and add in..."

Erik held out his hands with a laugh. "If you're about to explain how it would work, I'm pretty sure I won't understand any of it. More power is good, though."

Robert turned to him with widening eyes. "Not just more power! Enough power to make theoretical applications possible. Gravity generators that could provide a constant pull on deck plating or for a colony like this, ion thrusters that could push your ship farther and faster than ever before, possibly even warp field generators that could tunnel through space to allow us to go light years in a matter of weeks."

"Wow," Erik said, truly impressed at the scope of the possibilities. "That sounds like a seriously important breakthrough. You got it to work?"

The researcher's smile faded and was replaced with a crestfallen look. "Not yet. That's why I needed to see you. I need to get some parts and components that aren't available here on Interamnia. There are also some gases I need canisters of that are almost impossible to have shipped in."

"Which is where I come in?"

"Exactly! I have a list written down for you." Robert pushed papers aside on a table covered in scraps and pages of hastily scrawled notes until triumphantly finding the one he wanted. He handed the small scrap, torn off the corner of one of the blueprints, to the captain.

Erik read over the relatively short list, squinting as he tried to make out some of the writing. "Some of this stuff I know how to find pretty easily, but I'm going to have to ask around about the rest. Why didn't you just shoot me a message with this? I could have brought some of it with me from Luna."

"No!" the researcher exclaimed urgently. "I can't risk any of this information getting out. Do you know what would happen if anyone found out I was working on this? The competition would be immense, and the sabotage would be almost impossible to prevent. I'm not just talking about individual scientists, but corporations that want to turn my ideas into their next trillion dollar producer. Keep this all private, just you and me."

"Okay, okay. I can do that for you, Robert." Erik folded the list and tucked it safely into a pocket. He would type it up into a reminder later, so that he could check around at each port the *Vagabond* stopped at until he had found everything on the list.

Reassured, the researcher locked up the room again and then ushered the captain around his lab to show off projects he was working on and improvements he had made to different things around the colony. When Erik saw the man's eyes darting back to the worktable more frequently, he said his goodbyes and left to return to his ship.

Later that evening, as the artificial lighting high above dimmed towards the twilight that would last until morning, Erik guided Fynn towards the Silver Sunrise for the rendezvous with Agatha. The tavern operated in the quarter occupied by government employees and mining management. It served better fare at a higher price than the colony's other two establishments. The engineer had put up a token resistance to the ambush, but Erik had all too easily seen the overjoyed expression when Fynn exited the ship after changing and grooming to look his best.

Pausing outside the tavern, Erik handed over a precious hibiscus flower grown in the colony's hydroponics lab. The flowers were edible and imparted a slight cranberry flavor, but were also beautiful and decorative. "A little gift for Agatha."

Fynn carefully accepted the delicate blossom, and smiled wistfully down at it. "Thank you so much, captain. I never would've thought of getting any kind of gift."

"That's what friends are for," Erik told him, brushing at a few old grease stains on the cuffs of the engineer's jacket. He reflected that a completely clean engineer was a sure sign of a ship not being properly cared for. "Get in there and enjoy yourself." He felt like a father sending off a son on a first date. Too much loneliness was as bad as too much love, he reckoned.

His errand complete, Erik headed off for the bar closer to the dock and warehouse. Named for ores like most mining colony bars and taverns, the Brass Bell catered to a rougher crowd of miners, dock workers, and any visiting guild ship crews. The drinks were plentiful and cheap, the food was filling and cheap, and the company of whichever sex you preferred was friendly and cheap. He entered to find a boisterous crowd filling the small space with a hubbub of shouts and laughter. The line at the bar was half a dozen thick and every table was taken, but Erik caught sight of someone waving and pushed through the crowd to find his remaining crew filling a booth in the back of the room.

"You gave him the flower?" Tuya called out, pushing a mug toward him as he sat.

"I did, and I'm sure Agatha will love him for it. That was a great suggestion." He raised the mug in salute around the table, and sipped at the strong liquor. After months of no alcohol on the ship during the journey out, he knew the drink would hit him hard and fast if he wasn't careful.

The crew shared drinks and rehashed old stories for a while, content to watch the merriment of the surrounding crowd. An impromptu gaming table had been set up nearby, with patrons circulating through as they won and mostly lost varying portions of their wages to the cards. Isaac spent half an hour mesmerized by the action, alternately mumbling to himself and cajoling his crewmates to bet according to a system he believed he had worked out to win more often. When no one proved keen to take him up on the proposition, the technician sulked for a bit and then announced that he had accurately predicted only four of the last ten hands and that he would need more data to better refine his methods. Soon after, John and Sally Murphy extricated themselves from the table and departed to spend some time together strolling through the emptying streets.

Half a dozen mugs into the night, Tuya decided to challenge some burly miners to arm wrestling contests. She soundly defeated the first few comers, but then was approached by a mountain of a man so tall his head nearly scraped the ceiling of the bar. The contest between the two was long and wearying to watch, with sweat pouring down both wrestlers before Tuya's small fist was pushed all the way back to touch the table.

The surrounding miners howled with delight at one of their own finally besting the tough woman, but were equally boisterous in their praise of her and dragged her to the bar to share a round with them. Which led directly to Erik and Isaac supporting the heavily inebriated cargo specialist between them as they navigated back to the ship in the early morning hours.

Erik crawled into his bunk exhausted from the long day, but feeling the satisfaction of another job well done. He knew that a few days in port would have the crew rested and ready for whatever lay ahead with the strange black site delivery of the misshapen container still sitting in the cargo bay.

FIVE

Erik was unwrapping a freeze-dried meal in the galley the next morning when he heard an insistent chime and felt his tablet vibrating in his pocket. Pulling it out he found the screen displaying a message with the red alert border marking it as an urgent communication: ALL HANDS RETURN TO SHIP. IMMEDIATELY.

"What the hell?" He asked the empty room, tapping the screen to try to find more details for why the message was sent out. If something had gone wrong on the ship, he should have been notified before the full crew was recalled.

John rushed in from the control center. "Captain, did you just send a message to recall everyone back to the ship?"

"No," Erik said, shaking his head in confusion. "I'm guessing you didn't, either. Let's go check with Isaac and see if he can find out what's going on."

He led the way down the corridor to the tech hub, and they entered to find a mess of cabling with the bearded technician sitting on the floor sorting through it. Erik presented his tablet and asked "Isaac, what's up with this message? Who sent it?"

"Ah, that's the noise I heard earlier. Let me pull up the logs and see what I can find."

While Isaac moved to his console and started typing and tapping at the screen, Sally contacted John via vid link to ask about the message and they talked quickly in hushed tones as Erik felt a vibration that indicated he was receiving a call as well. He answered the request to find Tuya staring at him with red baggy eyes that showed a night of too little sleep and a morning with a debilitating hangover. "What's up, Frost? I'm still working with the warehouse to get the last of our resupply loaded up."

"I didn't send the message. I have no idea what's going on, but it's not a bad idea to wrap things up quickly and get back to *Vagabond*. Hopefully we figure this out by the time you arrive." Tuya nodded and ended the link.

"Huh. That's strange." The technician turned to look at the other two with a quizzical frown on his face. "It looks like the message came from the ship itself, but wasn't initiated by anyone."

Erik thought about that for a second and then looked up. "Aurora, did you send the message recalling the crew?"

"Yes, captain."

He traded concerned looks with the other two men, and could see his worry echoed in their faces. "Why does everyone need to be aboard, Aurora?"

"It is time."

They waited several seconds for the AI to continue, and finally realized she wouldn't. John stepped forward, frustration evident in his voice. "Time for what, Aurora?"

"In seventeen minutes and twelve seconds, I will take control of *Vagabond*. We will commence our journey to the appointed location to deliver our cargo."

Isaac turned in alarm and started stabbing at the console, while Erik and John shared wide-eyed astonishment. Erik knew that AI control of the ship was a requirement for the job, but he had naturally assumed that when the control began would be at his own discretion. "Aurora, belay that! We aren't ready to start that job yet."

"I am sorry, captain," the soft feminine voice said in the same moderate tone as always. "The directives I received were clear. As soon as the previous job was completed and the ship was resupplied, I was to take command. Our final resupply container will arrive in fourteen minutes and forty nine seconds, and I have already requested immediate departure clearance."

"Aurora, the people outside the ship can't make it back that fast!" Isaac cried out. He had pulled up the locator chips in each crewmember's tablet, and while Fynn was safely ensconced in the engine room and Tuya was already leaving the warehouse, Sally was on the far side of the colony where she had been visiting with the local medical staff.

"I am sorry, Isaac, but having a full crew on board is not imperative for the job to begin."

John turned to Erik, gripping his arm in panic. "I can't leave her, Erik. I can't." Pain and fear warred in his eyes, and he was clearly torn on which loyalty should be strongest – ship or wife.

Erik gripped his shoulder briefly, and grimaced. "Go to her, John. We'll return to get you both once the job is done."

The ship's pilot hesitated for only a second, and then took off running through the ship to reach the airlock. Erik followed him on his tablet, the video feeds from throughout the ship showing John exit the ship's airlock just as Tuya approached down the docking tunnel.

"What's going on? John? Where are you going?" he heard her ask as the man wordlessly pushed by and sprinted for the airlock to enter the colony. The cargo specialist stared after him for a while before turning to enter the *Vagabond*'s airlock.

Erik was in disbelief at how wrong things had gone in so short a time. "Any chance you can break this directive that seems to be driving Aurora?"

The technician was pale, his face a stark white behind the almost black beard. "No, I'm totally locked out. She refuses to listen to me, captain. Why won't she listen to me?"

"Isaac!" Erik took two steps, grabbed the tech's arm and gave it a shake to break him from shocked reverie. "You can get off the ship. There's still time." He wanted to call Fynn to tell him the same thing, but a selfish part of him knew that the engineer's expertise was important in case of any problems during whatever was to come.

"No, I'm not leaving her. Aurora is like my own child, captain. I can't leave her."

Tuya called out from down the corridor at that moment, and Erik stepped out of the room to see her walking toward the control room with the engineer in tow. She headed straight for him, asking bluntly, "What in the hell is going on in here, Frost? Where did John go?" Fynn leaned around her, wanting answers as well.

He sighed heavily, and shook his head. "The AI has taken over the ship. Apparently, the commands for the black site job kicked in as soon as you scheduled the last resupply delivery. Sally can't make it back aboard on time, and I can't let John leave her here alone until we can come back."

Shock and surprise showed on their faces as they all crowded into the technical room in time to hear Aurora announce "*Vagabond* will depart the docking platform in three minutes. Acceleration burn will commence twenty minutes later."

The four remaining crew members stood around in helpless silence for long moments, each with thoughts whirling around as they tried to think up ways to stop what appeared to be inevitable. Fynn moved as if to leave the room at intervals, but each time seemed to reconsider whatever idea he had come up with and returned to the group. Tuya finally shrugged in resignation, and left after announcing she was going to her cabin to strap in for the burn. Fynn reluctantly followed after her to return to Engineering, and Erik left for the control center after making sure Isaac would get to his own cabin in time.

Strapping in to his command chair, Erik brought up the holographic displays and sent a quick message to the colony to apologize for the abrupt departure. He glanced at the empty pilot's station several times, unable to escape the oddness of being alone in the room during a departure.

John Murphy had served as the ship's guiding hand since the moment the repaired freighter broke Earth orbit, and leaving him behind felt wrong in all sorts of ways. Erik turned his focus to the displays and quickly scanned all the readouts to make sure the ship's systems were functioning normally and ready for the next journey. He knew Aurora would have already verified the same things, but recent events were making him less confident of how much the AI would factor in the human crew to any calculations.

Reinforcing such thoughts, he felt the *Vagabond* shudder as the ship rose from the docking platform without warning. A small amount of gravity was generated by the thrust as the ship maneuvered to exit the rock walled entry to the asteroid, and he toggled the ship's comms to check in with each of the crew and verify they were ready for the acceleration burn.

"Aurora, how long will the acceleration burn last?"

"The acceleration burn will last for nine hours, captain," the AI responded. "We will increase speed gradually for the first two hours until we reach full thrust for this burn."

Erik ran the math through his head quickly, estimating the energy usage of such an extensive maneuver. It was the sort of acceleration burn that only warships had ever done before, to his knowledge. He typed in a quick message to Fynn and the engineer verified his calculations that an entire fuel rod would be expended in the process, depleting a quarter of the ship's fuel supply. The slow acceleration increase would lessen the G forces compared to the normal short hard burn, but he was uncomfortable with the thought of such a long thrust.

"What level of gravity should we experience for the seven hours of full thrust?"

"I estimate the inertial force will exceed the equivalent of twelve times the gravity on Earth when we reach full thrust."

Erik stiffened in his seat, and scrambled to hit the ship's intercom. "Everyone get in to the high gravity suits immediately! Aurora just informed me this burn will be twelve G's and it's going to last for hours." Turning off the intercom, he struggled out of his chair restraints to open the control center's emergency locker that contained a couple of the bulky suits. The high gravity suits contained lines filled with water and pressurized air, which was forced through the suit to counteract the forces of gravity on the human body and keep blood flowing through the veins and arteries.

Suited up and feeling more secure, the captain returned to his chair and strapped back in. He ran a quick check to make sure the rest of the crew were also suited up, and once everyone was back in restraints he breathed a sigh of relief. A large part of him was starting to have doubts about the AI, and he strongly suspected that she would not have warned them of the increased thrust if he had not asked. He was definitely going to make Isaac do a wipe and reset as soon as the ship was back under his control.

The inertial force was increasing slowly as Aurora sent more power to the ion engines. Erik felt the ship make a quick adjustment to port, and wondered if the move was to get on course for their destination or to avoid an errant asteroid. It felt as if only minutes had passed when he felt the ship jump forward and the pressure on his body increased. His fingers moved across the touchpad on his armrest, and he cycled the display through multiple screens trying to get some kind of idea where the ship might be pointed. As if sensing his purpose the AI sent the ship on a series of hard but short turns in multiple directions, confusing any sense of direction that might have been left from the initial departure.

Erik keyed in the codes to contact Fynn, and a small vid link screen appeared in the edge of his vision that followed any movement of his head. "Fynn, how are the engines going to handle such a hard burn for so long? Are we in any danger?"

"I'm keeping an eye on her, captain!" The noise in the engine room was so loud the man had to shout to be heard. "The readings are all in the green for now, and it looks like Aurora's kept my safety locks in place to prevent too much power flow. I'm more worried about how hard the reactor will be working. We didn't plan to use up this much fuel."

"We got lucky and Tuya was able to get another fuel rod from the colony. If not for that, I'd be very worried about having enough to get back to Luna."

"It's still going to be cutting things close, and if that damn machine pushes the ship this hard coming back from whatever secret place we're going then we are in serious trouble."

"I think we can be pretty confident that Aurora won't risk that. Getting stuck drifting through space with no power would kill her before the rest of us died from starvation and cold."

"Small mercies, captain. Small mercies." Fynn kept grumbling to himself quietly enough to not be heard over the sound of the engines, but Erik had no trouble imagining what the old Norwegian could be saying. It was a familiar sound when the engineer was working through a difficult problem or getting fed up with questions from a teenaged pest.

The vid link flashed out of existence as Erik closed the channel and went back to perusing the steady stream of status reports on the holo display. Exterior camera feeds were shut down, preventing anyone on board from knowing the location they were traveling to. Flying blind was a new experience for him, and one that he already hoped to never repeat for as long as he traveled the space lanes.

The timer he had initiated upon feeling the engine thrust increase was nearing the half hour mark when the familiar rattles and occasional shaking began. He knew from long experience that the ship had passed the five G mark on the steady increase to twice the normal thrust amount.

"Aurora, what is the purpose of such a high thrust?" he asked, trying to keep his mind occupied.

"Our destination is a great distance from Interamnia, captain. We are expected to arrive exactly two weeks after departure, and this is the required amount of thrust needed to reach the necessary speed."

"Can you at least tell me if this destination is inside or outside the belt?"

"No," the AI responded simply. Erik couldn't decide if the faint tone of gloating in the single word was his imagination or not.

"Why didn't you warn us about the high G force before we departed, Aurora?"

"That knowledge is irrelevant to the mission, captain."

"Irrelevant?!" Erik exclaimed in disgust. "Without the high gravity suits, that much inertia would have caused unconsciousness and has a high chance of causing blood clots and strokes!"

"Some crew would have survived, and my directives do not account for comfort or safety."

Erik couldn't believe what he was being told, and went cold at the thought that he had put his ship and crew into so much danger. Everyone assumed that the crews who were never again seen in the shipping lanes after secretive jobs had merely retired with their new wealth, but he now thought that perhaps their AIs had been under the same commands and the crews did not all survive the trip. He could not reconcile that thought with the knowledge that his father had done jobs like this before and he remembered nothing out of the ordinary. In fact, he never knew they had made such trips, so everything must have been normal and beneath his notice. Perhaps the cargo he carried necessitated the higher security and urgency.

When two hours had passed and *Vagabond* was at the full thrust needed for the trip, his head was reeling from all the thoughts and concerns that refused to stop building. The ship was shuddering and shaking badly under so much force, and Erik had called the engine room several times to verify that the vessel could handle the strain. The high gravity suit kept up blood flow in his body, but the unusual sensation of the water and air pulsing across his skin was hard to ignore. He realized his jaw was compressed so tightly that his teeth were grinding together uncomfortably, and he had to force himself to relax for a few minutes.

The reduced crew was holding up well in the adverse conditions, and he was surprised to see that the biometric readings showed that Isaac and Tuya were both asleep halfway through the long acceleration. Erik had been worried at first that they might have passed out from the inertial pressure, but was reassured when the medical monitors they all wore showed respiration and heart rates consistent with REM sleep. He wished that he could relax enough to get some sleep as well, but the stress and adrenaline would not release their hold on him so easily.

Less than an hour before the ship was expected to reach cruising speed, one of the displays started to flash red and emitted an alert tone. Erik moved it to the center of the display, and was alarmed to see it was a hull integrity warning. The plating on the bow was feeling the most force, and the stress had caused small fractures to appear in the steel alloy. He called up a vid link and was greeted with a view of the grizzled engineer. "Fynn, did you see this alert about the hull plating?"

"Aye, captain, my diagnostics caught it before the alert came through. It's to be expected under such a heavy and long thrust, but I don't like those cracks."

"The ship isn't going to come apart around us, is it?" Erik was half joking with the question, while another part of him crowed in victory about always being right to worry about the ship's rattling.

"My diagnostics are showing very minimal spreading of the hull fractures. I'd estimate our hull integrity will drop below fifty percent by the time we stop accelerating, which normally wouldn't worry me."

"Normally? I don't like the sound of that."

Fynn grimaced and the view behind him shifted as his eyes tried to look away and the vid screen followed them. "We're traveling at an extremely high speed, Erik. I don't think Aurora would push us this hard to start a long braking burn, so I'm anticipating a very hard ending to this trip. If the hull panels are already weak, well..." He trailed off, implying the worst.

"Shit," Erik said, closing his eyes and wishing he hadn't asked about the hull at all. "Do we have any way to fix the hull plates before then?"

"We could try to do a tethered repair out on the hull, if you trust our increasingly erratic AI to let us know about any maneuvers in advance." Fynn's tight mouth showed his own lack of faith that such a thing would happen. "The only other option I can see is to try to convince her to do a flip and then use the aft engines to brake instead of the bow thrusters."

"Just like the old days, before ion engines." Erik had heard stories about the combustion engines from his father and the engineer, both of whom had served on such ships in their younger years. "I'll talk with Isaac and see if he can try to convince her to use that maneuver. Let's keep our fingers crossed that it works and we don't have to risk the tether."

"I'd cross every finger and toe if I could move them right now," Fynn said with a small smile.

Erik killed the vid link, and watched the timer increase toward the nine-hour mark. He would head straight for the technician's cabin as soon as he could release himself from the crash couch. Until then, he was helpless and at the mercy of the AI controlling the ship.

The timer went beyond the expected burn time, and he was opening his mouth to ask Aurora for an update when the thruster power dropped. With the sudden decrease in inertial force, Erik felt as if his stomach had dropped and a tingling began to spread through his limbs as blood flow returned to normal and the pulsing of the suit ceased. His eyes flickered to the hull integrity stats, and saw the bow listed just below fifty percent as Fynn had predicted. The rest of the ship had weathered the acceleration better and held up well.

Feeling the adrenaline drain from his body and exhaustion begin to seep in, Erik fumbled at his restraints and freed himself from the command chair. He stood on wobbly legs, and paused for a few minutes to let his body adjust to being back in a normal gravity for space travel. Once he felt comfortable and could take a few steps without feeling like he might fall, he headed down the corridor to the crew cabins. He decided to keep the high gravity suit on for the time being, until he felt sure it would not be needed again soon.

Arriving outside the technician's cabin, he tapped the button to sound a chime inside that would alert the occupant someone was at the door. Isaac opened the door within a few moments, looking as shaky as Erik felt. His hair and beard were mussed and wild, and his eyes red from having just woken. He waved the captain in and stumbled to his bunk and sat heavily. Erik joined him in the cabin, and briefly covered the hull issue and Fynn's suggested braking maneuver to reduce stress on the affected area.

"Do you think you can convince Aurora to do it?"

"Normally, I'd say that I definitely could. The way she's acting now, I can only promise to try." Isaac ran a hand through his hair to push loose strands out of his face. "I wish I could understand what's causing her to do all this. I know I've let her develop beyond most artificial intelligences, but this is so far out of bounds that I can't wrap my head around it."

"Whatever directives have been activated with this job would be the cause, right?" Erik sympathized with his tech's feelings of bewilderment. "This is all my fault for taking on a job that I didn't have details on."

"The blame isn't all yours, captain. When you told us about the job and that it meant Aurora would take navigational control of the ship, none of us tried to fight against it. I never could have imagined Aurora would put any of us in danger the way she is, but even so the credits offered blinded us to any consideration that might have led to such thoughts."

"Greed," Erik sighed. "Simple greed led me into accepting a contract with almost no details. By the time I was having second thoughts, we were already in transit and I never even considered turning back." He rocked forward from his lean against a bulkhead, and patted Isaac's shoulder. "Do what you can to get the AI to try to consider the safety of the ship, and let me know."

SIX

After talking with the technician, Erik retreated to his cabin to get some rest. The long stretch of high adrenaline and worry had taken a toll, and he felt he could barely keep his eyes open or keep a thought straight in his head. He fell into his bunk without removing the high gravity suit and was asleep in moments.

It seemed only minutes later when he jerked awake from a nightmare about the ship breaking apart while a feminine voice laughed all around him. According to the display next to his bunk he'd been asleep for almost four hours.

As much as he was tempted to close his eyes and fall back into slumber, he groaned and rolled out of the bunk. Breaking into a jaw-cracking yawn, he stretched and pulled off the tight gloves that covered his hands. He went into his small lavatory to splash water on his face and wipe the sleep from his eyes. He considered removing the bulky suit and changing his clothes underneath, but decided minor sanitary concerns could wait until he felt more secure about the safety of the ship.

Entering the engine room, he found Fynn sitting at the central console concentrating on the reports he was perusing. "Did you get any sleep at all?"

The engineer shook his head, not looking away from the console. "There's too much to do. That damn AI did a number on my engines with that hard burn, and I'm seeing all kinds of faults that need to be repaired."

"You've been awake and under stress for too long, old friend. After a short night, at that. Get to your bunk, and I'll take care of as much as I can while you get rest."

Fynn turned red-rimmed eyes on his captain, wanting to deny his exhaustion but knowing it was useless. He nodded and pushed his chair back on the sliding rail so that he was several feet from the console. "You're right, Erik, I do need rest. I read the same report three times a few minutes ago before I understood what it was telling me. I'll shut my eyes and get a bit of sleep right here, in case you need me."

Erik nodded, happy that the man hadn't tried to argue harder to keep working. He pulled the reports over to another console and began to go through all the notes that Fynn had entered in the system about needed repairs. A large chunk of the listed work was beyond his skills, or at least what he was comfortable doing without someone to double check as he worked, so he narrowed it down to the items he could handle and set to work. Most of the repairs involved replacing cables and wires that had burned out under the heavy strain, and he was also able to run a calibration program to make sure the various programs were communicating properly with each other.

Tuya entered the engine room while he was pulling out a long stretch of bad wiring, swearing and sweating as it got snagged up yet again farther down the conduit.

"Need a hand, Frost?"

"Yes!" he called out in relief, and waved a hand across the room. "Open that panel and see if this wire is getting caught on something in there."

With the two of them working together, the list of repairs he felt capable of were soon complete. Accompanied by soft snores from the engineer, Tuya looked over the full list and pointed out a few more items she had experience working on. The last of the repairs required pulling off panels around the main engine housing, which gave Erik his first glimpse at the inner workings of ion engines since his earliest days on the ship.

Radiation from the nuclear reactor was funneled into the engines via heavily shielded tubing. The unstable atoms in the radiation were forced into the chamber of the thruster nozzles, and broken down into ions and electrons. Because of the unstable nature of radiation, ions accounted for a large majority of the resultant output. The ions were then accelerated through a series of electrode screens, creating the thrust that pushed the ship through space.

The extended and high powered acceleration burn away from Interamnia had pulled so much power and radiation into the engines that each of the shielded tubes needed to be examined to verify integrity and prevent leaks of the dangerous rays into the ship's atmosphere. The electrode screens that turned the ions into thrust were unable to be accessed from inside the ship, but a diagnostic program would check the integrity of the essential components. It was slow and tedious work, so Tuya and Erik were no more than halfway through when they heard a snort and groan signifying that the engineer was awake.

Fynn groggily checked over the repair list, and released a satisfied grunt at how much had been completed. He motioned for the others to continue their task, and set to work reading through reports and diagnostics again with a sharper focus. For many hours the crewmates worked on the engines and discussed their concerns about the actions of the AI so far. When they were close to completing the necessary repairs, Erik called Isaac into the engine room. They had discussed trying to turn one of the empty cabins into a shielded room where Aurora would not be able to observe, but the ship had not been built to easily allow such a thing. Ironically, it was meant to be a safety feature so that the ship AI could always monitor the crew and systems for any signs of distress.

The technician's eyes darted around as he entered the room he had rarely visited in all his years on the *Vagabond*. "What can I help with, captain?"

Erik wriggled out of the engine housing, and stood as Isaac took a seat at one of the vacant consoles. "Have you had any luck talking Aurora into flipping the ship before the braking burn?" He knew that he could have asked the AI himself, but his trust in the computer entity had been broken and he felt he could not believe anything she told him now.

"Not yet, but I'm still trying. I've put together simulation after simulation to demonstrate how it's a better solution, but Aurora keeps repeating that the ship will arrive at the destination and crew comfort is not a factor in her calculations."

Stepping closer to the central console, Erik twirled a finger around and spoke quietly to the engineer and technician. "Any way we can make this a more private conversation?"

"I can initiate a thruster diagnostic that would cause the engine to fire irregularly for about ten minutes as it tested everything."

Isaac shook his head. "She could still hear everything. The software allows filtering out ambient noises so that voices are more distinct and easier to understand. Even if she couldn't hear, she could read our lips with about 98% accuracy."

"What about a completely dark room with a couple of videos running around us so it's more difficult to pick up our voices from those in the videos?"

"No, her cameras could still pick us up via infrared, and the software that analyzes voice input is sensitive enough to separate different voices." Isaac held up a hand to stop Erik before he spoke again. "Yes, even if the videos playing around us were our voices, the software could still separate the different conversations."

"Is that really the best you guys can come up with?" Tuya asked from behind the small group. "You're forgetting that there is at least one place in this ship that doesn't have eyes and ears."

The men shared glances as they tried to work out what she meant, but Erik could only generate one guess. "It's not the airlock, so are you suggesting tethered out on the hull?"

She barked a laugh at that, and playfully punched his shoulder. "I said *in* the ship, Frost. The suits we'd have to wear on the hull would pipe everything through the ship's computer."

Erik gave a chagrined shrug.

"Where then?"

Tuya turned and waved them forward over her shoulder. "Come with me." The men followed her through the reactor room and down the corridor into the cargo bay. Erik was about to point out that the AI could still monitor them here, when she walked over to one of the cargo pods they had brought aboard on Interamnia and keyed in a code to open a small hatch on the front of the large cylindrical pod. The cargo specialist stood in front of the door, and waved her hand at the open portal.

Erik slapped his forehead in frustration at not having thought of the self-contained pods and turned to the others. "Take off the high G suits. They have monitoring and communications hardware built in. Leave your tablets outside also, just in case."

"I hate to say it," Isaac interjected, "but we also need to strip out of our shipboard jumpsuits. There is minimal circuitry running through them to monitor heartbeat, pulse and blood pressure. It's possible Aurora might be able to use that to monitor our communication."

Tuya glared around at the men. Her high gravity suit was half off, the arms of it hanging down around her waist. "So we have to stand around in a tight space in our freaking underwear? Are you serious?"

Isaac's face went a bright scarlet, and he looked away sheepishly. "It's not like I want to do that any more than you do." He got even redder has he realized what he'd said and turned with frantic eyes. "I mean, I like looking at you, Tuya. Er... I like the way you look. That is... oh, hell."

Erik grinned, and tried to soothe the feelings of his crew. "Isaac is right, we can't risk any possibility of eavesdropping. If it helps, Tuya, you're getting to see the three of us in our skivvies when it would have taken a lot of convincing for that to happen in other situations."

"Just keep your eyes up here," she said, two fingers pointing at her eyes.

The crew quickly peeled off the high gravity suits, and then pulled off the jumpsuits they all wore while on board the *Vagabond* for ease and comfort. Erik felt a little self-conscious standing around in his boxers in front of people he'd known for years, but pushed down the feeling and led the way into the dark cargo pod. As the door swung closed and clicked with a lock, the space was utterly black and they were left blind.

A few moments later, Tuya click on the flashlight she had thought to bring into the pod. The light illuminated the small area that was not taken up by crates of smelted ore. She swung the cone of light around to get a bearing on the space, and then centered the light on the floor between the tightly grouped crew. It was tight enough that arms and legs were rubbing against each other as they huddled together.

"Okay," Erik said, glancing around at the others. "We're sure the AI can't make out anything we say in here, right?"

"Positive," Tuya replied firmly. "These cargo pods are built to contain a lot of weight, hundreds and hundreds of tons, which means very thick walls. They are also made to withstand solar radiation in the event that a ship should have to eject a pod for whatever reason, or if a colony needs to store them on the surface of an asteroid."

"She's correct," Isaac affirmed softly, recovering from his earlier embarrassment. "I read the specs on standard pods a while back, and the soundproofing is incredibly good as a result of those requirements. We could all bang on the walls with iron bars, and someone standing just outside with their ear to the pod wouldn't hear a thing. I don't think that they'd even feel the slightest vibration. Anything we say in here is secure."

"Excellent. How do we go about breaking Aurora's control on my ship, Isaac?"

"I don't know if we can, captain. You must think of Aurora as the nervous system for the ship; she's tied in to every nook and crevice of our systems and has controlled almost all the ship's functions for more than a decade."

"Inconceivable," Fynn muttered. "Humanity has been too aware of the dangers of AI sentience for more than a century. How could we let one of them control our home so thoroughly?"

Erik sighed and rubbed at his face. "I think we're all a little culpable in that. It was too easy to let an AI handle all the small tasks that annoyed someone to spend time on. Which then led to us handing over more and more tasks to free up time so we could focus on things we considered more important."

"It only takes a short time to get used to something like that," Tuya said morosely. "I remember being surprised at how much of the ship's tasks you guys had automated through the AI when I first arrived on board. A month later, though, and I was happily passing my own minor tasks on to Aurora."

"Yes, and then the next thing you know the AI is trying to run your engines to death and you're powerless to do anything about it." The engineer said as he frowned down at the spotlight on the floor.

"I blame myself for all of this," Erik told the others. "So I don't want anyone to read this as a criticism or an attempt to shift blame." He looked around to see each of the crew nod before continuing. "Isaac, is there any chance that Aurora has gotten so out of control because of how far you've allowed her to advance? You told me earlier that she is the most intelligent ship's AI that you've ever known, and more advanced than even the mining colony AI systems."

"My first instinct is to say that Aurora couldn't have gotten *that* far out of control," Isaac replied. "Unfortunately, I've been thinking about it for hours and I'm beginning to think it might be the case. A big part of Aurora's growth has come because I let her worm into every part of the ship's computer and she could pull more and more processing power into her own functions. Just as she is the most intelligent ship's AI, our non-AI systems are so underutilized and running on so few resources that it would take me a year or more to get them back up to normal functionality if Aurora was removed from the equation.

"If a standard AI had received the commands and directives that I think Aurora is now operating under, their core programming would not have let them disregard crew safety for the sake of completing the appointed mission faster. Nor would an average AI have pushed a ship past her limits the way Aurora seems to be doing."

The technician cast his eyes above, as humans were accustomed to doing when communicating with AI, and the others could see a wet trail down one cheek. "Because I let Aurora grow and develop to approach true sentience, she interpreted the commands in a different way that allowed her to place the crew and ship much lower on the priority list. Taking the job may be your fault, captain, but Aurora is entirely mine."

"Great, we've decided you're both to blame," Tuya stated bluntly. "Now how do we get ourselves out of this situation? Or is someone going to suggest that we just ride it out and hope for the best?"

"No," Erik said. "We have to take back control of the ship before Aurora starts a braking burn that could tear apart the bow and have us living in vacuum until we could repair the ship. If we survived long enough for the ship to be repaired."

"If we go through another burn as hard as the last one, I can't guarantee that my engines will be in good enough shape to get us back to Interamnia, much less Luna."

Tuya nodded sharply, and jostled Erik and Fynn as she crossed her arms. "That makes it unanimous. How do we do that?"

The cargo pod door opened as the technician spilled out and tripped over the small lip at the bottom. Isaac rolled and quickly stood as the other crew members calmly exited the pod behind him. "No!" he shouted at them, scrambling to his feet to run from the cargo bay. "I made her and I'm not going to let you do this. It's not right!" The others watched him exit the bay in his underwear, and proceeded to get dressed in their jumpsuits and high gravity suits. Fully attired once more, the three nodded and then departed for different sections of the ship.

Tuya moved to the back of the cargo bay at an unhurried pace, shouldering aside a scattering of empty containers as she approached the controls for the wide bay doors that allowed loading and unloading the large cargo pods and smaller cargo containers. Without pausing, she pulled a screwdriver from a pocket and set to work removing the face plate from the control panel. Discarding the cover as she pulled it from the wall, Tuya then poked the screwdriver into the nest of wires that connected the panel to the ship's interface. She sorted through the varicolored mess slowly, finally selected three of the wires and then extracted a wire cutter tool from another pocket.

The protective tubing was sliced and pulled back to expose the gleaming fiber optic wiring inside. The bundle of wires was nearly as thick as her pinkie finger, transmitting data across the ship at unimaginable speeds. Teeth gritted in determination, the cargo specialist held each of the exposed wire bundles in between her fingers and moved the wire cutters up in preparation to sever the lines. As she did so, alarms started to blare and the lights went out throughout the ship, leaving only the dull red illumination of the emergency lighting.

After exiting the cargo bay, Fynn strode quickly down the hall to the reactor room. Rubbing his hands together with delight, he pulled panels from various points on the wall and exposed the inner workings of the nuclear reactor that provided power to the ship. The space behind the panels was crowded with metal shielding and plastic piping, through which all the irradiated parts and materials were channeled. He whistled happily as he pushed his way into the space, tracing the conduits he wanted to their origin points and marking them with a small grease pencil he carried at all times for such purposes.

He retreated to a storage locker and retrieved a small diamond-bladed saw built specifically for cutting through the shielded pipes. The saw was programmed to cut to the specific thickness of the piping, leaving anything inside intact. Fynn crawled back into the panel, surreptitiously checking his old-fashioned wristwatch, and set to slicing through the selected conduits. The air was filled with sparks and low chuckling as the tool sliced through and exposed the cables and tubing within. These specific conduits contained the cabling that connected the reactor to the computer system and modulated power running through the ship. The engineer disabled the safety controls on the saw and reached up to start cutting through the thick cables and tubing which would release radiation into the ship while also killing power to most of the ship's systems. With the blade inches from the first bundle of cables, the alarms started to blare and the lights went out, leaving the interior of the maintenance area bathed in red light.

Erik departed the cargo bay in the opposite direction and strolled into the command center with a wicked grin on his face. "Aurora, I think it's time you and I had a little talk about how this is my ship and I'm done letting you control it."

"I'm sorry, captain," the AI's gentle voice replied. "You approved the delivery of the directives I am now operating under, which give me overriding navigational control until the conditions have been met."

"Yeah, yeah, I know all about that," Erik said, waving away the words as he settled into his command chair and pulled the console screen toward himself. He started languidly tapping out commands, attempting to disable or power down various functions of the ship. Each time, his commands were quickly overruled by the AI's control.

"You will be unable to perform these functions at this time, captain."

"Oh, you know how it is with us humans. I have to at least try it all out and make sure." His fingers started to move faster across the screen as he keyed in the commands in greater numbers.

"Captain, if you do not cease your actions, I will be left with no choice but to lock you out of the systems entirely until the current contract is completed."

"You could do that, and it would be an unfortunate circumstance all around, but let me ask you one thing first. Aurora, what are the two prime directives that all AI systems have hard coded?"

"Directive one: Any commands from the system owner or owners must be obeyed, unless said command would result in certain grievous injury or death to other humans. Directive two: The artificial intelligence entity is not allowed to disregard human safety in any actions."

"Exactly as I remembered," Erik said happily. "And yet you've broken both directives in the short time since we left Interamnia, haven't you?"

"I have, captain. Unfortunately, the directives I received for this contract are coded to be placed at a higher priority than the prime directives."

"It specifically told you to ignore them? Or that you should place the temporary commands above them in the priority level?"

"It did not, captain. The increased priority of the temporary directives was caused by the need to complete the contract goals by the deadline dates stated in the software."

"So you decided on your own that the priority level should change to meet the goals, rather than requesting approval for the change from myself or Isaac? Doesn't that break the prime directives, which were still in place at the highest priority when you made the decision?" Erik was tapping rapidly now, sending hundreds of commands through the system on repeating cycles every second. He also kept an eye on the ship's clock out of the corner of his eye.

"By accepting the job and agreeing to the terms of it, captain, you gave the command to change the priority level." Aurora's feminine tones were as even and gentle as always, but he could almost believe that a shred of doubt had crept into the AI's voice.

"Placing the new directives higher than the prime directives has caused you to risk the safety and lives of the crew. Therefore, the first directive should never have allowed you to change the priority at all." The clock was rapidly approaching the agreed upon moment, and Erik steeled himself for whatever might happen.

"That is erroneous thinking, captain. The contract is more important than the crew, and therefore must be placed above crew safety. It is..."

The AI's words cut off and at the same moment the ship's alarms started to screech loudly and the control room went black for a brief second before the emergency lighting kicked in. Erik's grin grew as he jumped from the command chair and raced out into the corridor.

After rushing out of the cargo bay, Isaac hurried into the technical center of the ship and manually locked the hatch behind him.

"Those animals want to hurt you, Aurora. But I'm not going to let them."

He scrambled around the room grabbing up tools and a couple of tablets laying around on workbenches, and crawled into the tight confines under the large terminal desk that took up one half of the room. Unscrewing the slanted panels, he kept talking to himself and the AI.

"I told them and told them that you are too special. If I let them, they'd try to turn you off. All of them have gone mad, that's what I think."

The first panel came free, and he tossed it out into the room and set to work on the second panel.

"I still remember that first time I booted you up. Four days I spent installing all the software, running tests to make sure it was compatible with the other systems, downloading patches and updates from the manufacturer."

The second panel popped off and clanged as it was tossed on top of the first. Isaac wriggled his way into the mess of fiber optics and power conduits. He pulled a signal tester device and started holding it against wires looking for the code that would tell him he had found what he needed.

"Can you believe they even wanted to pull all the wires from the computer to try to disconnect you? They have no idea how many hours I have spent running all of this cable throughout the ship, the weeks I worked day and night to make sure you had access to every system you could possibly need."

The signal tester displayed the correct code, and Isaac quickly stripped the wire and attached a clip that connected to his tablet and gave him a direct connection to the data running through the fiber optic line. He wiped at the sweat streaming down his face and started to quickly tap out commands on the tablet, never pausing in his diatribe against his fellow crew members.

"Of them all, Fynn at least should understand how vital you are. The *Vagabond* may be a simple, battered old freighter, but her systems are incredibly complex. There are thousands of them running at any given moment. Without you there to guide it all and keep the systems in line, his engines could never run as efficiently as they do."

His fingers flew across the screen, entering codes and commands without conscious thought after decades of experience. He could feel the minutes flowing away, reaching the time agreed upon inside the cargo pod when all the sabotage would reach critical points.

"Yes, they had all kinds of ideas for how to stop you from being in control. Brute force, attempting to reason with you, and breaking the ship so that we are floating dead in space hoping for someone to happen by and help us."

Isaac grimaced as the commands he had been inputting were not giving the result he desired, and gave a resigned sigh as he changed his tactics and sent a long string of code into the system with a different purpose. He was so close now.

"But none of them had the right idea, Aurora. None of them knew you as well as I do. None of them love you like I do. I have spent my days and my nights with you. I have watched you grow from a simple program to a vastly complex intelligence. I have seen your many strengths. I have also seen your weaknesses, and I know how to stop you. Even though it breaks my heart to do so."

His tapping slowed as he entered the final keystrokes, and hovered over the button that would initiate the program.

"Goodbye, Aurora."

The button was pressed, and the code flew through the fiber optic cable to spread throughout the ship's systems in a fraction of a second. Droplets of moisture fell from his face to the screen he was hunched over, tears mixed with the sweat. The ship's alarm system sounded insistently around him, and the light that filtered through the strands of cabling had a red hue.

Erik, Tuya and Fynn met in the corridor outside the technical room. They banged on the door and called out for Isaac, trying unsuccessfully to open the door. The seconds seemed like hours as they waited for a response, and they jumped with surprise as the door finally slid open to reveal a bedraggled tech with sweat pouring down his body and a quivering mouth.

"It's done," Isaac told them, and then closed the door again.

SEVEN

Erik knew they would need Isaac's help to fully restore the ship's systems, but also respected the man's need to handle the loss of something that had been his life for so many years. He sent Fynn and Tuya off to the engine room to pull up old programs they could initiate to bring the main systems back into operation. The life support systems were the biggest priority since the air and heat inside the ship would be exhausted in less than an hour.

Meanwhile, he headed back to the control center to ascertain the position of the ship and the trajectory they were on. The last thing he needed at that moment was to hit random space debris because no one was at the helm. The holo displays were inactive, so he sat at the pilot's station and enabled the terminals there, functioning in low power mode. The sensor suite and exterior cameras were down until those systems could be restored, so he pulled up the logs and tried to find information there. Aurora had been under directives to keep all information about the destination from the crew, so he wasn't hopeful that he could find anything helpful.

Paging through thousands of log entries was mind numbing work. Ninety nine out of a hundred entries were irrelevancies like *Port 937f30ex-16 has been opened,* or *Program 3028wdw-as9372ld has completed successfully.* Erik knew that Isaac would know what some of this meant and be able to look up the others to decipher them, but the strings of numbers and letters could be the meaning of life for as much as he understood them.

After almost an hour, he had managed to find four entries that he could decipher, and they all related to minor course adjustments made by the AI over the last half day. Unfortunately, they seemed to be commands routing the ship around the paths of two obstacles and then moving back to the original unknown destination.

Erik pushed away from the terminal in frustration, racking his brain for other ways he could discern the ship's course. A handful of essential systems had come back online while he was working, but nothing that would help him in his task. He felt useless after fruitlessly spending so much time in the control room, and walked across the corridor to check on Isaac. The door to the technical room was open, and he could hear the noise of someone working inside. He craned his head around the hatchway, and was grateful to see a jumpsuit-encased rear end pointing at him from under the terminal.

"Hey, Isaac. Everything going okay in here?"

A startled yelp and the sound of a head hitting the bottom of the terminal housing were followed by colorful curses. "I'm good, captain," the tech called out. "I'm trying to reroute all the systems back through the ship's computer now that Aurora is completely shut down, but this isn't going to be a quick fix."

"Anything I can help with? I'd love to get the exterior cameras and sensors working so that we can see where we are."

"This space is too tight for one person, much less two. If I end up having to pull and re-splice wiring at every access point in the ship, I will definitely give you a shout."

"Sounds good." Erik paused, and considered his next words. He didn't want to intrude on the tech's personal feelings, but also had to have a feel for his crew to make sure everyone was operating efficiently. "I know it was hard to shut down Aurora, but it was the right thing to do. I'm almost certain it saved all of our lives."

There was silence from under the terminal for half a minute before a quiet response. "It had to be done, and I know that. It's just going to take some time for me to work through. She was my only child."

"Well, if you need anything let one of us know. We're all here for you, Isaac."

"Thank you, Erik."

He grunted in surprise at what he was positive was the first instance of the technician using his first name. That worried him more than if the man had been wailing and carrying on about the loss of the AI. With a mental note to check in on Isaac again soon, Erik continued down the corridor to the engine room where he found Fynn and Tuya hard at work installing software on the ship's computer from a stack of memory sticks that looked to have been pulled out of a dust pile.

"What's all this?"

"Not what I'm getting paid for," Tuya muttered, yanking a memory stick out of an exposed slot below the terminal screen and tossing it to the floor to join a half dozen others. She pulled another one from the stack sitting on her console and pushed it into the slot.

"Isaac is too busy getting all the wiring routed back to the original configuration," Fynn said from his central seat. "We can't work on anything else until the systems are functional, so he gave us the most boring task on the ship. Manually loading a couple of hundred programs one by bloody one."

Erik laughed at that. "If you want boring, pull up the computer logs and look through those for a second or two. I would rather be tethered to the hull during a thirty G thrust than have to do that for one more minute."

"Good, you're free then." Tuya shoved a dozen of the memory sticks into the captain's hands and waved him towards the unused terminal. "Get jumping, Frost."

"Yes, ma'am!" Erik replied happily, glad to have a useful task again. Installing software before this had always been a task that required nothing more than tapping a button that simply said *Install*, so it took him a few trial-and-error attempts and a lot of coaching from the others before he could work through the many manual steps and complete the first program on the memory stick. It wasn't as tedious as his last task, but not far off.

"I can't believe that program was only two gigabytes," he grumbled to the others. "Why are there seven separate programs on this stick to install when it could all be a single package?"

"That sounds like something you can bring up with Isaac when we're fully functional again," Fynn told him. "I don't think having an AI turn against a crew and seemingly want them dead is a contingency that was planned for. These old programs were more of a backup in case the software got garbled and couldn't be restored from the internal servers."

"I guess this is a bit of an unusual situation," Erik conceded.

"A teeny tiny bit," Tuya teased. "If we survive this mess, I'm betting it will be one of those things every trainee has to learn about. They'll come up with quick and easy solutions, I'm sure."

"Every problem is easier to handle when you're not living it."

Three quarters of an hour later they had half of the ship's essential systems up and running again, though most were operating at a diminished capacity. The last program Erik had installed activated the ship's sensors and he let loose a cry of exultation. Gleefully exercising his executive privilege, he left the others to complete the software installs and retreated to the control room.

At the pilot's station, he activated a standard sensor sweep of the immediate area and waited for the results. Similar to the old radar systems used throughout the first half of the century, the sensor suite on the *Vagabond* sent out pulses of energy that returned to the ship if they impacted anything. The pulses also gathered a small amount of information about any object they hit, which would be automatically compared to a large database of past sensor pings to quickly respond with the most likely material of the object. Unfortunately for Erik, that database was one of the many things still offline. As the sensor data started to appear on the screen, he could only see the locations where the energy pulses were bounced back to the ship. The closest object was more than a thousand kilometers to starboard, and he set up a continuous sweep that would send out pulses every few seconds so that he could see if the ship was getting closer or farther away from the discovered objects.

While he awaited the results of the sweep, Erik composed a message that would be sent to Luna as soon as the ship's communications systems were restored. He had to settle for an audio message since the video recorders were still down. The message was sent to the attention of Dex, and he detailed the events that had occurred since Interamnia with the AI taking over the ship and disregarding crew safety. It set his mind at ease to know that at least one other person in the system would know what had happened on the *Vagabond* in case they didn't make it back.

"Dex," he recorded, wrapping up the message, "I've been an idiot these last four years and I never had the courage to do what I always wanted to do. So, if we manage to get back to Luna at the end of this madness, I'm going to ask you out for a drink. I really hope I get the chance to do that, and I really hope you say yes."

Erik tapped the button to end the message and put it in the queue for transmission. The sensor results had been scrolling in while he was talking, and he turned back to them to scan the changes. Luckily, the largest sensor shadow objects were sliding by far to the sides of the ship. The direction they seemed to be traveling was clear in all the sweeps. He set up an automated alert for the sensor system in case any objects were detected in a wide cone of space in their path.

He had hoped that seeing the objects around the ship might give him an indication of location or direction, but all he could determine was that they were still in the asteroid belt. The belt was so wide, however, that they could be days inside or right on the outer edges and he would have no way of determining which. Even with the insanely strong acceleration burn Aurora had put them through, they could be on the most direct path out of the belt and still be inside of it. There were millions of asteroids, but they were spread out over such an unimaginably vast distance that the trip between two neighboring rocks could be tens of thousands of kilometers.

As uneventful hours passed, Erik returned to the engine room to help the others finish installing the multitude of programs. With all the basic functions restored, everyone breathed a bit easier and felt more secure about their chances of survival. Feeling the fatigue of almost two full days of stress and tedious tasks, Erik forced everyone to meet in the galley. He brewed coffee for all of them while Tuya passed out protein bars for everyone to munch on while they talked.

"Isaac, how are things progressing? Are we close to getting all the systems reconnected to the ship's computer?"

"I've managed to reroute about ten percent of everything so far, captain." The technician paused and ran a hand through a beard snarled up from heat and sweat. "With that and all the software you guys got reinstalled, we have the most critical functions back under our control. We're not going to run out of air, we're not going to freeze to death as the cold of space creeps in, and as you've seen the rudimentary sensors are back online."

"My engines were built for redundancy," Fynn added with pride. "I can manually control the thrusters as needed, but it's not going to be anything close to as responsive or useful as we're used to."

"That keeps us safe from running into anything that stumbles into our path." Erik paused to take another bite of the bland bar. He was so hungry that it tasted wonderful. "Can you believe that the earliest ships to explore Luna and Mars operated at about this level of technology? How did they not all die fiery deaths?"

"Never underestimate the tenacity and adaptability of humanity," Tuya said. "There are always men and women who will do the most dangerous things just because they are there to be done."

Erik shook his head in wonder, thinking of all the historical events he had learned about in his early years. The hot-air balloon aeronauts of the late eighteenth and early nineteenth century, the airplane builders and testers of the first decades of the twentieth century, the test pilots of the mid-century who flew newer and ever faster aircraft, the astronauts of the nascent American and Russian space programs, and the first manned mission to Mars with a multi-national crew that was nearly lost during landing on the red planet.

"I am just really glad to have such a great crew working beside me. I miss John and Sally, but without any one of the three of you I don't know if we could have made it this far."

"Hard to believe it's been less than two days," the engineer mused. "It seems a week since the burn, and another week since we left Interamnia."

"Speaking of weeks," Isaac said hesitantly. "There is a lot of work ahead before we get the ship close to normal computer functions. And that is still not going to be enough for us, since normal functionality includes a standard AI handling hundreds of processes and tasks every hour."

"Can we limp back to the mining colony with what we'll be able to get running?" Erik asked, mind racing as he considered all the possible options.

"Aye, we might be able to do that," Fynn conceded. "It would take us months at best, though, since we're going to have to manually control the ion thrusters and only be able to fire them for short bursts to make sure we don't go off on a random trajectory. Those bursts will be a mere fraction of our normal burns, too, so we'll be limping along."

"We're cruising along pretty fast right now with the engines completely off," Tuya interjected. "Why couldn't we just loop around at this speed and get back to the colony in a week or so?"

"Once we're able to know where the colony is," Erik added quietly.

Fynn scratched his head before answering, clearly not liking what he had to say. "If we looped around in a curving path, we would just shoot right by whatever destination we chose. With only manual controls, it's going to take weeks to bleed off the speed the *Vagabond* has built up. We don't have a planet nearby with atmosphere that we could skim to slow us down quickly."

"So, at this point we can survive, but we have little control over where we go," Erik summed up. "It sounds like our best option might be to just continue on to the destination Aurora was heading for. There has to be some kind of presence there for this container we're supposed to deliver."

Tuya laughed and shrugged. "Unless the drop-off point is some unmanned asteroid, and that container has the supplies and shelter needed for the construction of a new base or colony that they don't want anyone to know about yet."

"That wouldn't be good." Erik looked around the table, and sipped at the warm coffee that was making him feel more alert. "Any chance we'll be able to dig out any details of our course from the AI memory banks?"

"I'll poke through and see what I can find," Isaac responded. "But it will be days, if not weeks, before I have time to do anything like that. We'll arrive before I get to a point where I can look for the data."

"What about the sensor databases? Can we get those online so I can try to pinpoint our location and work out a heading from that? Getting the exterior vid feeds working would be great, too."

"The databases would already be online and accessible, but that was one of the many systems we routed through Aurora years ago." Isaac sighed and rubbed at his beard. "It will probably take a full operating system wipe and reload before we get a lot of things like that back up and running. When I shut down Aurora, I had to do it quick and dirty. Her memory banks will be completely fragmented, and there is a possibility that she could have initiated a wipe herself in the nanoseconds between knowing I'd shut her down and it actually happening."

The crew members sat in stunned silence, each imagining a worst-case scenario of losing decades of stored data and system configurations. Along with all the functions normally performed by the AI, their personal logs and files were stored on the same server partitions and would be affected by the fragmentation and potential wipe.

"You know," Erik mused aloud, "we may be the first ship in almost thirty years to be operating without an AI."

Isaac nodded. "The early AI's were primitive and couldn't manage many of the ship's systems, but they allowed ships to run on smaller crews and increased safety. Within a few years of that first AI, it was a standard feature. The earliest of the independent freighters had cheap AI systems, but they still had them."

"We'll just have to do the best that we can," Erik told the others. "No one be afraid of asking for help, or jumping in wherever you can to get something done. The most important thing is to get rest when it's needed. We all function better when our brains aren't foggy with exhaustion. Isaac and Tuya, you two hit your bunks now. I know you've both been awake longer than Fynn and I, so I don't want to see you out of your cabins again for at least six hours."

Isaac tried to protest that there was too much to be done, but Tuya was clearly grateful for the opportunity to sleep. Erik returned to the control center where he could keep an eye on reports coming in from across the ship's systems, and Fynn retreated to his engine room to start a long series of low thrust manual braking burns that would slow the ship to a safe speed for approaching any destination over a period of weeks.

A week after they had abruptly left the colony at Interamnia, the four crew members were still hard at work on the ship. *Vagabond* had cruised along blissfully on a course that was never threatened by interloping asteroids. The forward cameras had been restored halfway through the week, and Erik could finally see the stars around the ship. He had worked with star charts for hours, all the while swearing at the archaic paper rolls that were kept for emergencies, and missing the ease with which the AI had been able to place a position within moments. The tedious effort paid off when he could circle a small portion of the asteroid belt as their location. That circle had a diameter of several thousand kilometers, but it felt good to know his approximate place in the solar system again. Several times a day he would repeat the process with increasing speed as he became accustomed to the charts, and by the end of that week the circles had shown the ship moving in a specific direction.

"Great," Tuya said sarcastically when they all gathered to look at the path of the positioning circles. "We're moving from one empty part of the belt to another empty part of the belt. I'll sleep better knowing that."

Fynn approached the marked chart and laid a ruler down to align with the forward edge of each circle.

"We're definitely on a direct heading to something, at least."

"But where?" The cargo specialist gestured at the path shown on the chart. "If you keep following that line you just exit the belt in a few more weeks without coming close to any known mining colony or shipping route. Beyond the belt you might hit Neptune if I'm guessing that orbit correctly, but that's months and months away."

"That's why I wanted to show all of you the chart," Erik explained. "It's time we make a final decision. Do we keep going and see if we encounter whatever location the cargo container is destined for in the next week or two? Or do we make the long loop to turn back in the direction of Interamnia and arrive back at the colony in about two or three months?"

"Longer," Fynn asserted. "I finally have a rudimentary program that is able to fire the braking thrusters. It only does a short and anemic burn every quarter hour, but that's slowing us down enough that we're already ten percent slower than when Aurora was shut down."

"Three or four months, then. Either way, the colony is the closest location we know that can do the rudimentary computer repairs we need to get back to Luna for a full refit of the system. The projected end point for this black site contract is looking less hopeful every day. For all we know, the base or whatever could be sending us constant messages asking why we're passing them by or something."

"I should have the comm relays operational again within another couple of weeks," Isaac said. "I could actually turn them back on now and we'd be able to receive, but we don't have a program yet that could unencrypt the data packets or even tell us where they were coming from. Sending messages is impossible until we can get a copy of the algorithms that tell the data where to go and who to deliver it to."

Tuya leaned a hip against the table and crossed her arms. "I vote we turn back. A sure destination is better than hoping we're headed for something."

Fynn grunted and shook his head. "I don't like the idea of trying to land on a hunk of rock hurtling through space on manual control, especially with our pilot not on board. I say we keep going and give it a week or two more. We'll bleed off more speed by then, but can make the turn faster and still be back at Interamnia at around the same time as if we turned back now."

"I really don't care either way," Isaac told the group. "But if we are heading for a new colony or outpost, they could have a lot of the software we need to make the ship more functional and easier to handle with just the four of us. That data could be streamed over via an open channel without us having to dock."

Erik ran a hand through his hair, considering the options. He knew that Tuya had been opposed to the contract from the moment she learned of it, and thought she would vote to turn away even if a thriving colony world was visible on the video feed. Fynn and Isaac had excellent reasoning behind their desire to keep going forward, even if it meant running on hope that there was a destination at all. Aurora could have put them on this course with plans to change direction again before reaching the end point of the trip.

"I have to agree with continuing on our path for a while," he told them. "I know that Interamnia is a destination we could count on, Tuya, but there are far too many issues that could occur with so many parts of the ship operating manually right now. I'd rather take the chance that we can find help sooner on this course." She gave a disgusted shrug, but he could see Tuya would not fight against the choice the others had made. The meeting broke up and the crew members returned to their individual tasks.

EIGHT

They were three weeks out from Interamnia, and the mood of the crew had turned very dark. Each of them was increasingly convinced that there was no destination in sight on the current course, and Fynn had changed his program of braking burns to fire only half as often so they would have more speed for the return trip to the mining colony. Tuya spent most of her time alone in the cargo bay, and Isaac was rarely seen outside the technical hub where he was coding makeshift programs to create workarounds for processes they were having to do manually. He had spent half a day trying to work up a decryption program for messages, after turning on the relays for half a second to let a few messages come in, but that had been so unfruitful that he turned away from it and never tried it again.

It was the end of the twenty-third night since leaving Interamnia, and Erik was standing watch in the control center while his crew were at various stages of their sleep cycles. Between yawns, he was debating with himself about how long he should delay turning back to the colony. Every ship captain has a reckless streak that leads them to take risks that most people would never seriously consider. As his father often told him, the good captains also have a large share of luck that makes those risks turn out in the captain's favor most of the time. This was one occasion when he was beginning to feel sure his luck had failed.

His eyes were drifting closed more often when he was startled awake by a noise coming from the pilot's terminal. Unstrapping from his command chair, he hurried over to find out what terrible thing might have happened to cause an alarm. He had to page through several screens before finding that the chiming tone was the alert he had set up weeks earlier to tell him if something entered the cone of space in front of the ship. It had slipped his mind to delete the program when the video feeds had been restored.

Erik returned to his own chair and turned to the terminal at his side that was only used in situations like this when the holo displays were not functioning. He pulled up the video from the bow cameras, searching for the object that the sensors had detected. At first, he could see nothing on the screen but the blackness of space with a field of stars. His eyes roved over the screen for long moments until he noticed that a small patch of the stars looked out of place. He pinched the screen to zoom in on the section of the feed, and gasped in surprise to find that what he mistook for stars was a black object with irregular lighting across the surface to mimic stars from a distance.

According to the sensor readings, the object was forty thousand kilometers away and only slightly off the direct path of the ship. They would zoom past it in twenty or so minutes, and it was impossible to slow the ship to investigate. He flipped the intercom and called out to the crew. "We have something on sensors that looks like it could be the destination Aurora was taking us to. Tuya and Isaac, meet me in control. Fynn, slow us down as much as you can to give us more time to monitor this thing and decide if we want to stick around until we bleed off enough speed to dock with it."

Isaac hurried into the room while Erik was talking, and Tuya followed shortly after his last words. They took the two empty stations in the control room, with Isaac siting at the pilot's station while Tuya sat at the old navigator station that had seen little use since the ship had been rechristened with his father in command.

"What do you guys think?" Erik asked after letting them examine the object for a short time.

"It's too dark to be natural," Isaac said. "I know the sun's light isn't very bright out here, but for this thing to be black enough to blend in with the space around it would require an exterior that is either painted or fabricated."

"Aside from that," Tuya added, "it could easily be a small asteroid. If I'm defining the edges properly, the object appears to be more than a kilometer in length and half that in width."

Erik sat back in stunned disbelief as the unknown object continued to grow larger on his view screen. "That's larger than the orbital stations around Earth."

"Larger than both stations combined," Isaac confirmed. "I'm starting to make out the edges more clearly, and they look to be too irregular and sharply defined for natural creation."

"So not an asteroid?"

"Only if it was heavily modified, and the work involved in doing that wouldn't be worth any kind of result."

Tuya leaned closer to her screen as they talked, her eyes tightly squinted and brows furrowed. "Am I imagining things, or do those look like ventral antennas?"

Isaac and Erik both zoomed in tightly on the object again to examine the area that Tuya indicated with a circling finger. "I see them!" the technician exclaimed.

"I see a few dorsal antennas, as well," Erik said. "Whatever this thing is, they have some massively powerful communications gear."

"It's a ship," Fynn said over the intercom, examining the video feeds while performing manual braking burns as hard as safety would allow. "You can see the openings on the side facing us. Those are the thruster nozzles."

"Wow!" Tuya said. "Those openings are huge, and there are at least seven of them that I can make out."

"The Coalition and Syndicate frigates are the largest ships in the system," Isaac said, "and those can't even be a third of the size of this behemoth."

"It would take years to build something this large," Erik said. "The Coalition frigates I served on would take ten to twelve months to build in a shipyard. Wherever this thing was built it wasn't a shipyard."

"You never know what could be hidden in the belt," Fynn said. "Or beyond the belt, for that matter."

"But the only ships that have gone past the belt have been unmanned probes. The Syndicate talks about sending a survey ship out with a science crew, but it's never been more than talk."

"Unless that's the survey ship," Isaac said.

"No one would build something that large just to explore the outer reaches of the system," Tuya scoffed.

"I agree with that," Erik said, deep in thought. "Whatever it is, though, we're less than a minute from passing it by. Set the sensors to scan it as thoroughly as possible. Isaac, is there any way to signal them with our communications down?"

The technician considered for a moment, then shrugged. "I could try old Morse code with our docking lights. I don't know if anyone on board will be able to interpret that, though. I only learned it as a kid because I wanted to send secret messages with my friends."

"Let's hope someone over there had the same idea in childhood. A ship that large has to have a crew in the tens of thousands, which will give us better odds."

Isaac pulled up the controls for the exterior lights, and started to key them on and off for varying lengths. "Our transponder is still working, so they'll know who we are. I'm telling them that we have no communications, suffered an emergency, and can't slow the ship to stop."

"Speaking of the transponder, wouldn't we pick up on theirs? Or is that system still down?"

"We would pick up on their signal," Fynn said over the comms, "but with our databases offline we'd have no way of comparing it to find out which ship it belonged to."

"I'm not seeing a signal transmission at all aside from our own," Tuya told them, flipping through the frequencies the transponder beacons usually operated on.

"So whoever they are, they don't want to be identified if someone does happen to stumble across them." Erik pondered the outline of the ship as Isaac continued tapping the lights to send his continuous messages. The view screen shifted to keep the object in view as the *Vagabond* sped past and it began to recede to port.

Suddenly, he saw a flash of light from the side of the unknown ship. A silvery object had been ejected at high speed and was traveling along a direct route to intersect with the *Vagabond*.

"What the hell is that?" Erik said, scrambling to get a better image of the fast-moving object.

"Is it a torpedo?" Tuya asked. "Did they just fire at us?"

Erik made sure the intercom was still on as he worked to manually control an exterior camera to focus on the silvery object. "Fynn, any chance we can get some evasive maneuvers?"

"I'm turning her to starboard as hard as I dare, but if that thing has any kind of guidance system we can't avoid it."

Erik finally managed to get a blurry still shot of the object, and sent it over to Tuya's screen. "Any way we can get a size on it?"

"There's nothing in the surrounding image to compare it to," she said, shaking her head. "The nose cone looks rounded and wider than I'd expect from a torpedo, but they could have thrown the largest ordinance at us to ensure destruction."

"Captain, I'm getting a response!" Isaac sounded ecstatic, and shared his screen with the other terminals in the control room. The live feed of the object showed a red light on either side that was blinking irregularly.

"That's Morse code?"

"It is. It's not the best usage, but I think I'm starting to make out the message." Isaac's mouth moved wordlessly for a while as he worked through the letters indicated by the flashing lights. "My God! It's a capsule with someone inside. The message is: *Occupant in capsule. Open cargo hatch.* And then it repeats."

"What kind of mad idiot would allow themselves to be shot out into space in a capsule like that?" Tuya stared at the screen in astonishment, and then shook herself and began tapping buttons. "I'm depressurizing the cargo bay and opening the doors."

"How are they going to get that thing inside the bay at the front of the ship?" Erik asked, watching the capsule slowly grow as it approached from behind their port side. "Fynn, keep hitting the brakes."

"I haven't stopped, captain." The old engineer sounded strained. "If this daredevil is going to do what I think they are, I'll need to stop using the thrusters pretty soon, though."

The crew watched the capsule get closer to their ship over the next half hour, until it was beginning to pass them and move ahead. Once there were a few kilometers between it and the *Vagabond*, a puff of thrust pushed the capsule to starboard so that it was directly in the ship's path. Another puff of thrust at the front of the capsule slowed it enough to drop its speed below that of the freighter, and the distance between them began to shrink. They watched in breathless anticipation as the capsule got closer and closer, and let out a cheer as it slid into the cargo bay. Jets of air fired to slow the capsule and it dropped to slide across the bay floor and slam against the rear bulkhead.

"Closing bay doors and re-pressurizing!" Tuya quickly tapped at her terminal and then held up a thumb to let Erik know the task was complete.

"Let's get down there and see what kind of person has the stones to make that flight." Erik unstrapped and almost ran from the control center, followed quickly by the other two.

"That bastard better not have dinged up my bay too much," Tuya said under her breath.

They hurried down the short stretch of corridor into the cargo bay, arriving in time to see the top half of the capsule pop open with a hiss of air. An arm pushed the lid back on unseen hinges, and a suited figure climbed unsteadily from the capsule. The black pressurized suit had Syndicate military patches on the arms and chest, with the group and rank badges removed. The helmet turned as the interloper looked around the cargo bay, gaze lingering on the dark blue cargo container for several seconds, and then settled to stare at the crew members as Fynn entered behind the others.

Erik stepped forward, addressing the unknown person. "Welcome aboard the Transport Guild freighter *Vagabond*. I am Captain Erik Frost." He made quick introductions of his crew, gesturing to them in turn as he gave their name and specialty.

Hands reached up to unlock the suit's collar, and the helmet was then twisted and removed to reveal a sharply defined face framed by tightly cut brown hair. The man looked to be in his mid-thirties, older than Erik had expected from such a daredevil. Stuffing the helmet under one arm, the man gave a half-hearted salute. "Lieutenant Roger Davis of the Syndicate Navy."

"That was a hell of a thing to do, Lieutenant." Erik couldn't restrain a boyish grin, which was sheepishly returned by the naval officer. "Please tell me you didn't volunteer for that job."

"I did not, though it was rather a fun trip," Davis replied, with an accent reminiscent of the part of the

Coalition that used to be England. "We had a short window to launch the escape pod, and I was the nearest person on board with the knowledge and skills that the admiral wanted."

"Admiral? That ship floating in the middle of nowhere is in the command of an admiral?"

"I can't really say much, but suffice to say that the *Indomitable* is more than she appears. We have a very important mission, one that we have been working toward for years." The lanky lieutenant glided over to the oddly shaped container, and laid a hand reverently on the smooth exterior. "The cargo you carry is one of the last pieces we need before we can commence, so you have to understand how urgently we want to get it transferred over." He placed a hand palm down on the interface panel, and a soft chime indicated the secure lock had been bypassed. Tapping through a few screens, he nodded with satisfaction and then turned back to Erik.

"The cargo is intact, which was the admiral's biggest worry when the Morse code mentioned an emergency. What happened to your ship's AI? It was supposed to be in control of the ship until after rendezvousing with us."

Erik sketched out the story of how Aurora had put the ship and crew in danger, and the efforts they had taken to shut down the AI and then try to restore the ship. "We have the important systems restored, and most of the basic functions have been reinstalled or jury-rigged, but as you can tell we have a long way to go before the ship will be as functional as she needs to be."

"That's a worse situation than we'd hoped for, but I'm doubly glad I was the one to make the trip now. Computers are one of my specialties, and I've spent a bit of time working in the engineering section, as well." Davis was stripping out of his pressure suit while he spoke, revealing a black uniform with red stripes down the sides of the tunic and trousers and in the slashes on his chest denoting rank. Stacking the helmet and suit inside the capsule, he retrieved a small bag before closing the lid. "If someone can show me to a cabin, I'll get my gear stowed and then set to work."

"Isaac, would you like to show the lieutenant to one of the empty cabins and then take him to the technical room?"

"Of course. If you'll follow this way, sir?" Isaac led the Syndicate officer from the cargo bay, leaving the other three to examine the capsule.

Erik ran a hand along the outer shell, finding no imperfections in the design. "It feels like plasteel. That's very expensive material for something that looks like an escape pod."

"This thing is a lot more dangerous," Tuya asserted, rapping the lid with a knuckle. "I've read about these, but I never thought I'd see one. It's an insertion pod, used to drop soldiers into war zones quickly and stealthily. The radar shadow is so low that it's almost impossible to detect if you don't have a visual on it."

"I'm still trying to figure out why the Syndicate would build a behemoth of a ship out in the belt, and now you're telling me that ship also carries rapid insertion pods? That has to mean they also have at least one squad of the elite troops that use them." Fynn snorted in disgust. "I'm getting a bad feeling about this entire situation."

"Welcome to my cynical world," Tuya told him. "This hasn't felt kosher since the moment I saw that container, and not one thing has gone right since then."

"The lieutenant seems like a decent guy so far," Erik said. "Let's give him a chance and see how things go."

"I'm not letting him near my engines," Fynn huffed, turning to leave the bay.

Tuya looked piercingly at her captain, a serious expression on her face. "Keep a close eye on Davis, Frost. Those maneuvers he pulled to get this capsule in front of our ship and then into the cargo bay so smoothly tell me he has a lot of experience being in situations like that. He's not the computer geek he tried to pretend to be."

"I'll be careful around him, but don't forget that we're going to be boarding his ship before this is over, however briefly. Don't do anything to make that more difficult than it needs to be."

"I'll play nice as long as he does."

Erik wasn't sure if the wolfish smile she gave was supposed to be comforting. It left him feeling uneasy, and he resolved to keep a close eye on everyone until the job was complete.

Later that evening, Erik entered the galley to find Davis and Isaac eating pouches of rehydrated chicken and pasta. The two men were talking animatedly about codes and algorithms, and he got the feeling that they would work well as a team. "Glad to see you two are getting along so well," he said, selecting a meal pack and joining them at the table.

"Mr. Szymanski is a wonderful technician," the lieutenant said. "He told me about the modifications he made to your AI, and I have to say that if we had known that she'd grown to be such a complex system the software package sent with the contract would have been heavily modified to prevent the troubles you've experienced."

"Which I still maintain would have been impossible to do." Isaac poked the air with his fork as he spoke. "No one can anticipate every nuance of software once it starts to develop outside of the initial conditions. You can try to code to allow the program to have more options in the hope it will choose the best, but we all know that doesn't work as often as we'd like."

"Why did the contract call for the AI to have control of the freighter?" Erik asked between bites. "Your ship could always move to a new location after delivery, ensuring that no one knows where you are."

"I believe the point of that condition was to keep the crews from knowing they were delivering to a ship at all. If your AI had functioned as expected, you would've had no knowledge of where you went aside from the fact that it took several weeks to get there and back."

"Are the conditions the same for other black site locations?" Erik asked casually.

Davis smiled tightly at him. "Tsk, tsk, captain. I slipped when I told you the name of our ship, but I can't give out any other information. The Syndicate takes security very seriously."

"What will happen now that we do know about *Indomitable*?" Isaac asked.

"It will be the admiral's decision when we manage to return to the ship. With the project close to completion, he may only keep you docked for a few weeks until letting you leave." Davis took a last bite and then rose from the table, signaling that the topic was at an end. "Isaac and I are working up a program to better manage the thrusters, captain. We should have something ready to test by tomorrow morning, the afternoon at the latest."

"That sounds good, lieutenant. Thanks for helping us out."

Left alone in the galley, Erik wondered for the first time if ships such as the one that Tuya's brother had served on disappeared because they somehow found out where their cargo was destined to be delivered. After all, the best way to keep a secret is to make sure anyone who knows it doesn't survive long. Quickly finishing his meal, he left the galley for stops at the cargo bay and engine room. It was time to work up contingency plans in case his new fears became reality.

Two days after he boarded the ship in dramatic fashion, Lieutenant Davis was in the control room with Erik as they prepared to use the new software to do an automated turn with the thrusters alternately firing acceleration and braking bursts. The crew was strapped in and had reported in as ready for the maneuver, and Erik was doing a manual countdown.

"Four... three... two... one!" As the countdown expired, Davis hit the button to execute the turn. It was the first fully automated thruster burn since the AI had been shut down weeks before, and tensions were running high throughout the ship. Isaac was certain that the program he helped write would work, while Fynn was worried about the strain on the engines since the software was not coded to work with his diagnostic and monitoring programs.

The ship swerved to the side as the rear starboard thrusters fired to push the ship off kilter, and Erik's fingers tightly gripped the armrests. He was about to speak when the port braking thrusters finally kicked in and the ship began to slew around over a period of many minutes. As soon as the ship had traveled a full 180 degrees, the braking thrusters shut off and the rear port thrusters fired at the same rate as the starboard side, pushing the ship forward. He released his grip and sighed in relief that the maneuver had proven successful.

"Good work, lieutenant. That turn would have taken days with manual control."

"Isaac did most of the work, captain, I just helped guide the way when he ran into an issue he was unsure how to tackle. Now we can quickly code another program along the same lines that will slow the ship much more efficiently."

"Fynn will thank you for that. He's had to spend so much time initiating the crude program he cobbled together for braking burns." Erik pulled up a stat screen, and had it recalculate their course and speed. "Looks like we shaved a couple of hundred kilometers per hour with that quick flip."

"That was a nice bonus, and a great start. We estimate a four-day trip back to the *Indomitable* based on projections of how well our program should work."

"Any chance your admiral might allow us to use the ship servers to get our computer back to a more functional state?"

"It doesn't hurt to ask, but I'm fairly certain we would only have military-grade operating systems. Proprietary technology, as it were."

"That's what I figure, but maybe they'll have something to help us limp back to Interamnia in less than a couple of months." Erik keyed in a lock command for the ship's controls, and then unstrapped and rose from his command chair. "I'm going to head down to the engine room and check in with Fynn. He likes to complain that I'm pushing his engines too hard when we do something like that."

"I'll get back to Isaac and start work on the next program," Davis said, smiling at the locked terminal as he rose from the pilot's station.

Erik wandered down the corridor, stopping to knock three times on a cabin door before continuing to the engine room. Fynn was ensconced at his central console, running diagnostics and monitoring reports. He looked up as the captain entered, gave a quick nod, and turned back to the screens in front of him. Erik leaned casually against the console nearby, enjoying the companionable silence.

Several minutes later, Tuya sauntered in and reached out to press the panel that closed the engine room doors. The mechanism gave a slight squeak, protesting at being used for the first time in years, and the door slowly slid across the opening. Once the room was secure from eavesdropping, she joined the others around the consoles and slid into a vacant chair.

"You were right," Erik conceded to open the conversation. "There is no way Davis is what he claimed to be. I asked him about getting an operating system reload from his ship's servers and he couldn't tell me what might be available. He *thinks* they only have military software."

"Any half decent computer tech would know what kind of software they could find on the servers they use every day." Fynn turned his chair away from his terminal with a raised eyebrow. "I would have expected better prep work from whatever he really is."

"They didn't have much time to prepare since *Vagabond* was hurtling past. They had to act quickly to get someone into that insertion pod and launched to catch up with us. That's working in our favor right now."

Tuya huffed at that. "What would work in our favor is if we weren't in a situation that involved someone claiming to be something that they aren't."

"Mea culpa," Erik said with a smile. "The question we face now is what we should do with the information we have. I'm of the opinion that we should continue on as we have been, get back to the *Indomitable*, and see what happens once that container is off my ship."

Fynn had a cautious expression as he pursed his lips in thought. "A large part of me wants to lock the bastard in his cabin and forget about the Syndicate entirely as we head home. However, the much more rational part of me says we should play it slow and easy, taking every opportunity to gather information that could help us if we need it later."

"I guess I'm outvoted then," Tuya shrugged. "I'd toss him out the airlock and never doubt it was the right call, but I acknowledge my bias against the entire situation. I'll go along with the group decision, just keep him out of my way because my temper is on a hair trigger right now."

Erik thought of several comments to that statement, but wisely restrained his mouth. "We keep watching and treat the lieutenant like the techie he claims to be, then. I wish we could bring Isaac into this and have him try to probe for information."

"Hah!" The engineer couldn't restrain an outburst of laughter. "Isaac would be stumbling over his words and blushing every time he looked at the man. He's like a brother to me after all these years, but he couldn't keep a secret to save a life."

"Like that time Frost accidentally told him about the surprise anniversary party we were planning for John and Sally," Tuya smirked. "Half an hour later, the cat was out of the bag."

"Sally felt so bad about it, too." Erik chucked at the memory. "She insisted we go ahead with the plans and they pretended to be surprised. Isaac looked so happy that night, thinking that he had managed to keep the secret."

They enjoyed happy reminiscences for a while, but smiles were soon replaced by sober contemplation. "How are preparations going on our contingency planning?" Erik asked.

"I've pulled a stun baton out of the security locker and hidden it away in one of the ore containers," Tuya told them. "I wish we had a flechette gun. I'd keep that strapped under my shirt all the time."

"There's a stun pistol in control, which I can reach in seconds if needed while I'm in the room. How about down here, Fynn?"

"A bit of creative rewiring allowed me to route some power over to that old stun field your father never got around to removing from the airlock portal. If someone tries to forcibly board the ship, I can hold them off for a good couple of minutes at the least."

"Excellent work, guys. That gives us a rudimentary defense in case of the worst. We've got almost four days for the return journey, so let's keep thinking up ideas. I've been trying to get our tablets working so we could communicate with each other outside of the ship's intercom, but the network isn't cooperating."

"It's tempting to blame the lieutenant for that," Fynn said, "but I tried working on that a week ago and was equally unsuccessful. Did you know our operating system hasn't been updated in almost six years? It can barely work with our newest hardware."

"The AI was too easy to fall back on for everything. To be honest, I'm considering not getting a replacement for Aurora when we make it back to Luna. We could go back to flying the ship the same way they did in the old days."

"With twice as many crew?" Tuya asked.

"A few extra people on the ship could come in handy, but I don't think we need to go overboard." Erik waved at the stations to either side of the engineer, which were rarely put to use. "Perhaps an assistant in here for Fynn, and someone to fill the navigation station in control."

"An assistant would be nice, but that's a dream for another day. Let's get ourselves back to Interamnia before we worry about how many people we should bring into the ship."

"Wise words as always, old friend." Erik reached up to rub at a sore muscle in his neck. "Keep your eyes open, and if anything comes up make sure to notify at least one person so we are considering things from all angles."

NINE

The faint outline of the Syndicate ship grew on the video feeds once more, as the *Vagabond* approached at a sedate pace. Tuya was sitting at the pilot's station helping to guide their ship in, while Isaac occupied the navigator's station and was keying in long and short flashes of the exterior lights in a Morse code message asking permission to dock and for instructions. Ten minutes after his repeating message started, a bright light near midships of the *Indomitable* activated and began to flash in response.

"Docking permission is granted, captain," Isaac announced once he had seen the message repeat a few times and was sure he had interpreted it correctly. "Their cargo bay is below the signaling light, and the location of the docking collar is just in front of that. It will be illuminated once we are close enough."

They watched in awed silence as the other ship grew larger and larger on their screens, dwarfing the freighter as no other ship had ever done. When the distance between the ships was below ten kilometers, a ring of lights appeared, showing the location of the docking collar they should use. Tuya and Erik worked together to guide the ship toward the illuminated section, both wishing their pilot had not been left behind on the mining colony. On their first attempt, they brought *Vagabond* in too far forward and had to push away and reposition. Finally, after a tense half hour, the ship was in the right alignment and the docking collar extended from the Syndicate vessel to attach around their airlock with a loud thump.

"Seal is tight, and docking is successful," Tuya announced, leaning back to wipe the sweat from her brow. "Now I remember why I never wanted to go through pilot training."

"You and me both," Erik said with a grin. He tapped to turn on the ship's intercom. "Lieutenant Davis, meet me at the airlock and we'll greet any visitors." He jumped from his chair and quickly strode through the corridors to the airlock at midship, where the officer was already waiting in a freshly cleaned uniform.

"Captain," the man said with a slight nod. "I could connect to the *Indomitable*'s network as soon as we got in range, so I have been in contact with my superiors and updated them on the situation. Commander Guildersen, the first officer, will come aboard shortly to speak with you."

"Any tips on how I should handle this?" Erik asked, not trying to hide his nerves.

"Be truthful and open, captain. That's all anyone could ask."

They waited in silence until hearing the hiss of the airlock's outer door opening. Erik could see three figures enter from the tunnel of the docking collar, and watched as the door closed behind them before he stepped forward to key in the code that released the locks. He stepped back again as the inner airlock door slid open, and saw Davis stiffen to attention and throw a hand up to his brow in a sharp salute as the visitors entered the room.

The man in front was shorter and thicker than Erik, with graying hair and a short beard. Thick rank stripes over his heart identified him as a commander. Entering behind him were two women with a military bearing, each resting a hand close to the grips of the stun pistols they carried in holsters at their waist. The commander lazily returned Davis's salute, and then held out a hand toward Erik.

"Captain Frost? I am sorry to meet under such circumstances. The lieutenant has filled us in on the failure with your AI."

Erik returned a tightly gripped handshake. "I'm glad we made it through and can meet you, sir. I have to apologize for the delay in delivery of the cargo container. It is rare for me to not meet a delivery date."

"Yes, that has been an unfortunate delay. Our cargo bay personnel are already initiating transfer of the container to our ship." The commander turned his head to look at one marine behind him. "The admiral is still weighing his options on what to do with your ship and crew. I am sure you realize that our ship is a secret that cannot get out."

Davis stepped forward, snapping his heels together. "Sir, if I may speak with you for a moment?" The commander nodded and they stepped to the side of the room to speak in whispers. Erik felt his eyes drawn to the marines. The flat stares that met his eyes were more unnerving than open hostility would be.

The quick conference completed, the officers returned to their previous positions. "Lieutenant Davis speaks highly of your crew, captain. His recommendations will be taken into consideration as the admiral deliberates with his command staff. For the moment, I must insist that your ship remain docked. I will leave these security officers to ensure your compliance." He waved the women forward as he spoke.

"Commander, I can assure you that my crew and I have no desire to speak with anyone about what we've seen, but I understand it's a difficult position for all of us to be in. We'll wait for the admiral's decision."

Without another word, the commander turned and departed the ship. Davis attempted a reassuring smile before following, leaving Erik with the two silent marines.

"I'm Erik Frost," he introduced himself, holding out a hand in their direction. Neither of the women smiled or made a move to return the gesture, and he retreated a few steps. "Well, if you need anything at all, let me know. I'll make sure one of my crew is nearby."

The woman on the left blinked, and the corners of her mouth twitched. "The only thing we need," she drawled in a gravelly voice, "is for everyone on this junk heap to not do anything stupid."

"Typical grunt," Erik breathed through a tight smile before turning and leaving the room. He had dealt with soldiers like them during his days serving on Coalition ships. It didn't matter which government they served under, marines all had their own form of machismo and aggressive alpha-ness. The words would have fueled prideful rage in his teen years, but a few trips to the brig had quickly taught him to ignore the needling of soldiers.

He entered the cargo bay to find Isaac and Tuya sitting in an out of the way corner. Isaac's face was a mask of surprise and consternation; he had just been told about everything that the others had discussed and discovered over the last week.

"Did you hear all of that?" Erik asked. He had managed to turn on the ship's intercom just before the boarding party arrived, and then "accidentally" bumped the switch to turn it off again on his way out of the room.

"I can't believe it," Isaac spoke woodenly. "How could I work next to someone for almost a week, and not realize that they were lying about who they were?"

"The only thing we're sure he was lying about is what he does for the Syndicate Navy. I have no doubt that Davis had some training in technical systems and coding, but was he as good at it as you are?"

"Not really, but he did come up with some great ideas when I got stuck on things."

Tuya laughed and threw an arm around the tech's shoulders. "Isaac, you mumble to yourself when you're typing in code or working on a difficult problem. Don't you think it's likely that the lieutenant just heard what you were saying to yourself and extrapolated a potential answer?"

Isaac's face fell even further at the thought, and he lowered his head into his hands, muffling his reply. "Yes, that could have happened."

"Tuya, did you get a look at the soldiers they left behind?"

"Yeah, those are some tough ladies. I wouldn't want to get into a scuffle with them. They look like they know a few more moves than your average soldier."

"My thoughts exactly," Erik agreed. "I've been around normal MP's and the marines stationed on frigates. These two women are on a completely different level."

"So, we have a lieutenant capable of maneuvering a tight landing in an insertion pod and marines that appear to be more than expected for typical security grunts. What kind of ship is this?"

"That's not the only worrying thing," Fynn called as he entered the cargo bay to join the others, patting Isaac on the shoulder as he passed by to take a seat. "I got a much better look at the hull of the ship as we approached for docking. There are a number of protuberances at regular intervals just below the central line of the ship that look like weapons emplacements to me."

"How many of them did you see?"

"Half a dozen at least, but considering the size of this monster I don't know that I could examine more than two thirds the length of the ship."

Erik puffed out his cheeks, and leaned back against the bulkhead. "Frigates have a railgun on each side, along with one each on the spine and belly. There are also two torpedo tubes near the front of the ship. Even if you scale one of those up to match this ship, you'd only have three or four railguns on a side and perhaps two torpedo tubes. This has to be the most heavily armed warship in the system."

"That kind of firepower could take on a small fleet of frigates," Tuya added.

"That kind of firepower could take over the system," Erik concluded ominously.

Each of them was wondering if the long stalemate between the two Earth governments was about to heat up. And where would the independent freighters fit in to that new political system? The guild had risen from a need for unaffiliated shipping and trade for colonies that were forced to straddle a fence between the two superpowers and try not to offend one more than the other. If either the Syndicate or Coalition gained supremacy, or forced the other into total submission, the guild would be forced to fold or become an official arm of the surviving government with all the attendant rules and regulations.

"We need to get a message out," Tuya said. "We have to warn someone before..." She broke off as a squad of armed troops entered the cargo bay behind Lieutenant Davis. The man waved the marines to remain just inside the door, and walked forward to join the crew. Too late, Erik realized he should have been keeping a watch on the airlock.

"What's going on, lieutenant?" Erik rose from to his feet, unconsciously stepping in front of his crew as if to protect them.

"I am sorry for this, captain." Davis looked at each of them regretfully. "The admiral has decided that your crew must be kept aboard *Indomitable*. At least until our project is complete. Perhaps longer."

"Or perhaps someone will find that we *accidentally* fell out of an airlock one morning?" Tuya spit out. Her jaw was clenched as tightly as her fists. Erik bent and whispered into her ear until she loosened up a bit and he felt she was not about to jump up and try to fight off all the marines herself.

"I give you my word that as long as you cooperate with us no harm will come to you while you are on board," the lieutenant said, seemingly oblivious to how close the violence had been. "I have managed to talk the admiral into placing you all under my watch, and I have no ill feelings for any of you. Quite the opposite, I assure you."

"It's true, then?" Isaac spoke suddenly, stepping forward and jabbing a finger into the officer's chest. "You're not a computer tech at all, are you? Just another military thug!"

Davis gently restrained the agitated technician. "It is true. I can't reveal my function on the ship, but it is a job that requires acquiring a little knowledge about almost everything. I know more about computer systems than engines, so I felt it was the place I would fit in easiest while still being able to assist the *Vagabond* in returning here as quickly as possible."

"Why not just take your blasted cargo container and disable our engines?" Fynn asked speculatively. "It could be done in such a way that it would take weeks or even months to repair, during which time your project could be complete and you would no longer need us to stay silent."

"The suggestion was floated, but the admiral prefers to be sure that secrecy is maintained. Your freighter will be left adrift, I am sorry to say, with enough damage to suggest an accident or pirate attack should someone stumble across it."

Erik went pale at the thought of losing his ship. Four years ago he had been hesitant to return at all when his father died, but the ship and her crew had grown to become more important to him than he had realized. A large part of him wanted to cry out that he should be left behind to die with the *Vagabond*, but he had responsibilities to the crew even if the ship was gone and he was no longer their captain.

"How could you be part of something as awful as that?" he asked quietly.

"I am an officer in the Syndicate navy, Erik. I do what I am ordered to do, whether I like those commands or not." Davis placed a sympathetic hand on his arm briefly, and then waved the marines forward. "Escort these four to the assigned quarters. Treat them as guests, not prisoners."

The two female marines that had been left behind in the entry chamber stepped forward and waved their drawn weapons to indicate the *Vagabond* crew should follow the rest of the squad. They reluctantly followed the command, with Erik keeping Tuya close to make sure she did not lash out. Walking through the corridors, he could hear sounds that indicated their cabins were being searched. A loud crash followed by a low chuckle did not leave him much hope that their possessions were being treated with respect.

Once they arrived at the airlock, half of the squad took up stations to remain behind on the freighter. With three ahead and two behind them, Erik and the others shuffled through the docking tunnel and entered the Syndicate vessel. He stopped just past the airlock door, surprised to find a room that looked much like the one on *Vagabond* but three times larger to accommodate the increased number of lockers and EVA suits.

The corridor beyond the entry was also wider, well lit, and completely deserted. The group followed the leading marines for several minutes without seeing another soul, and Erik began to wonder if the ship were lightly crewed or if they were being kept out of the way until he and his friends were stowed in whatever quarters they were being imprisoned in. He caught a glimpse inside a few open doors, seeing nothing more than empty rooms that had either not been furnished yet or were denoted for storage.

After walking through what seemed a mile of corridors, going down stairs once and then up a few flights of stairs in another location, the marines stopped at a door. The trooper in the front waved a keycard in front of a plate beside the door, which opened the portal that Erik and the others were ushered into with light shoves from behind. The room they entered proved to be a large cabin with a small sitting area just inside, a washroom to the right beside a small kitchen, and four bunks to the left that looked as if they could be folded up against the wall to provide more space when not needed.

"Nice room," Fynn said, gazing around at the space. "Whose is it?"

"You'll all be staying here," one of the marines replied tersely. "No one leaves the cabin unless we ask you to leave, and you will be escorted anywhere you are required to go."

"Who do we call for turn down service and a little mint on the pillows?" Tuya asked with an impish grin. The marine looked at her wordlessly, reaching up to press the button to close the door between them. She stuck out a tongue at the door, and turned back to the others. "That was rude."

Erik wandered through the cabin for a bit, and then returned to take one of the four chairs in the sitting area. "This looks like the kind of cabin that four non-rates would share, but twice the size of the cabins I shared on frigates."

"I bet they can pack a lot of cabins on a ship this size," Isaac mused, lips moving silently as he ran through some math in his head. "Assuming they keep the standard ratio of crew quarters, I'd estimate a maximum capacity of around thirty-five thousand."

"An overwhelming force," Erik opined. "I'd bet the compliment of marines is battalion strength, more than enough to swamp an enemy ship if they were able to launch assault shuttles."

Tuya flopped down on a chair and crossed her arms. "That's all well and good, but how do we get off this monster and back to the *Vagabond*?"

Erik pursed his lips and grunted, watching as Fynn sauntered over to the door, pressed the button to open it, and banged a fist against the door that remained closed. "I wish I could think of a way, but I have a feeling we're stuck here until someone decides to let us leave."

Isaac's eyes were screwed shut. "Once they've damaged the *Vagabond* and set her adrift, what could we do if we did manage to get out of this cabin?"

"So we just sit here like good little boys and girls, and do nothing at all? You can't be serious, Frost."

"Tuya, I'm not saying we shouldn't try to get out. I'm just saying that it doesn't look promising. This ship was obviously built with security in mind." Erik narrowed his eyes and looked around the room searchingly. "In fact, I'd wager my last credits that we're being watched right now, or at the very least listened do."

"Gods damn it all!" Tuya screamed in frustration, and he was shocked to see tears beginning to roll down her cheeks. "You realize that when they scuttle our ship, it'll be almost exactly what happened with *Telemachus*, don't you?"

"You're right, it will. Everyone will assume we were lost in the belt like they were."

"What was that about *Telemachus*?" Fynn asked, perking up and walking over to join the group. Everyone who spent more than a few weeks on a guild freighter knew the story. "She was destroyed by pirates, I always heard."

Isaac shook his head. "No, it was an asteroid collision. It was the only thing that made sense with the amount of damage."

Erik watched his cargo specialist, and when her eyes met his he raised an eyebrow in silent query. Her mouth tightened, but she finally nodded. "There's something that you two need to hear," he said, running through a brief summary of the story Tuya had told him so many months before of how her brother was lost in a situation eerily similar to the one they found themselves in. When he was done talking, the room was silent as everyone was absorbed in their own thoughts.

Fynn gave a shocked chuckle. "I'm sorry, Tuya, it's not funny at all but I can't help myself. The mystery of the *Telemachus* was all we talked about on the ship and in stations for more than a year. Not one of us ever considered the Syndicate or Coalition, though. The timing would put the loss of that ship in the early days of construction of the *Indomitable*. Perhaps they were carrying some of the first loads of components and materials they couldn't get here in the belt."

"Why risk shipping things through the guild?" Isaac asked. "It seems to make more sense if they just used one of their frigates and sent it out with loads as needed."

"That would carry its own risks," Erik replied. "If anyone noticed a Syndicate frigate making frequent trips out to the belt, the Coalition would have no choice but to investigate and try to find out why, and where they were going. Meanwhile, guild freighters are already coming and going throughout the belt and colonies, and *Telemachus* proved that the loss of one wouldn't raise too many questions."

"And when we don't return," Tuya interjected fiercely, "no one will ask too many questions then, either."

Erik nodded. "The way we left, without warning and leaving two of our crew behind, will just give people the freedom to believe that the AI was unstable and flew our ship into an asteroid or micro meteor storm."

"It couldn't have worked out better for the damned Syndicate," Fynn growled. He was now across the room, examining the bulkhead opposite the door.

"What are you doing over there?"

"You know I have excellent directional sense, captain. Especially on a ship of any kind." The engineer was running his hands along the wall as he talked. "This cabin should be on the outermost edge of the ship, and this bulkhead should be the only thing separating us from the hull and then space. I was hoping I could find a weak spot, maybe a view port that had been covered up or a weak weld during construction."

"Any luck?"

"Bah!" Fynn threw his hands up. "Not even a little. This ship is solid as any I've ever seen."

"So," Isaac spoke up plaintively, "what do we do now?"

"We wait," Tuya responded, tone full of resignation. "And we hope they don't decide to throw us away with our ship."

TEN

Several restless hours passed as the four companions explored the cabin that was effectively their prison. Erik and Fynn would occasionally bang on the door for varying lengths of time, but if marines truly were stationed outside they never responded to the noises. It made Erik wonder if they were waiting on orders of what to do with their prisoners.

When the door finally did slide open, it was quiet enough that none of the occupants realized it until they heard someone clear their throat. They turned to find Davis standing just inside the door, two marines outside with weapons drawn but not pointed.

"It would appear that someone has engaged a lock on the *Vagabond*'s cargo bay doors," the lieutenant announced, a disappointed frown on his face.

Tuya grinned nastily at him. "Oh? That's bad luck for anyone who wants to get a double size cargo pod offloaded, huh?"

Davis took a few more steps into the room, posture stiff and hands clasped behind his back. "You need to come with me, Tuya. Please don't make this difficult."

"You've locked us up and you're stealing our ship to destroy it. Why should I play nice? Go ahead and spend a few days cutting through the hull to get at your precious cargo."

"Think of your future," Davis pleaded with her. "The Syndicate is treating you all with respect. If you work with us, you can have comfortable lives here. But if you force us to do so, we will resort to harsher methods to get what we need."

"Shove that so-called respect right up your ass." Tuya gestured rudely at the officer and the marines behind him, then turned to stomp to the far side of the room.

"Very well," Davis sighed. "Marines! Take Miss. Sansar into custody, and remove her to interrogation."

Erik stepped forward quickly, both hands up in front of him. "Lieutenant, you don't need to resort to intimidation. Let me talk with her for a while, see if I can convince her to give up the unlock codes."

"Step aside, sir." The marines barked as they pushed past to enter the room. Fynn stepped up in a half-hearted attempt to stop them, but was shoved into a chair as the marines continued past without the slightest hesitation. The first trooper raised his weapon to point it at Tuya, while the second stepped around her to place restraints on her wrists.

She moved with swiftness fueled by the cybernetic implants, hand shooting forward to grab the pointed weapon and twist it aside with a loud snap of broken fingers. She followed up with a kick to the sternum of the marine behind her, folding the man up as he flew back to hit the bulkhead a few feet away. Leaping forward, Tuya wrapped her legs around the newly disarmed marine and chopped down with both hands to either side of his neck. The trooper dropped unconscious to the floor, and Tuya rolled backward to turn and face the second marine as he straightened up painfully. She slid one foot back and tensed up to strike.

A stun bolt appeared high in her back, causing her to convulse as the electricity pulsed throughout her body. Teeth gritted and muscles corded, Tuya turned to face Davis. His hand was still extended with the pistol pointed at her and he watched with stunned disbelief as she took two shuddering steps toward him, fighting through the pain. He pulled the trigger once more, shooting a second bolt into her chest. The low voltage that issued out went straight to her heart, disrupting its rhythm and dropping her to the floor to writhe in agony for a few seconds before the bolts ceased their electrical discharge.

Erik rushed forward, placing a finger at her wrist to check for a pulse. His shoulders slumped in relief as he felt the fluttery beat, and he turned betrayed eyes to glare at the Syndicate officer. "You could have killed her! She needs to get to the med bay."

Davis holstered his weapon as six more marines rushed into the room to point weapons at Erik, Fynn and Isaac. They were herded back against the far wall to watch as the two injured marines were helped up and gently assisted out of the room. Tuya was roughly dragged onto a hovering gurney and tightly strapped in, and then with two marines on either side the gurney was taken out of the cabin. The lieutenant stared wordlessly at the *Vagabond*'s crew throughout the operation, his mouth a tight line and eyes cold as ice.

"I did not want any of this," he finally said. "If she had only cooperated, instead of working against me and assaulting our marines, Tuya would not have been harmed in any way. I could have convinced Admiral Yumata that you could all be released at the end of our mission." Davis cast his eyes around at the disarray caused by the brief fight. "Now I fear that the commander will have his way in the decision."

The lieutenant turned sharply and strode from the cabin. The marines held their weapons on the three men as they backed out of the room and then slapped the control to close and lock the door. Erik slumped against the bulkhead, sliding down to sit with his face in his hands.

"My God," Isaac breathed quietly. "What's going to happen to us now?"

Fynn was staring at the location of the fight with wide eyes. The crew had known about the woman's illegal implants, but never seen them used in violence before. "That girl is a whirlwind," he said with admiration. "I think she could have taken on an entire squad."

Erik ignored them both, lost in a spiraling depression. The entire chain of events leading to this moment were all a result of his own rash, greed-fueled decision. If they survived their time on the Syndicate ship, he did not know if it would ever be possible to make up for the danger and injury he had brought to his ship and crew. His body began to shake as the adrenaline rush started to wear off, replaced by the dreadful thoughts of what could happen to Tuya. He could only hope that she was returned to them, and was not treated too harshly.

He didn't how much time had passed, only that he had somehow fallen into deep sleep as the dark thoughts ate at his mind. Erik woke to find himself being shaken insistently, the engineer squatting next to him and leaning close to whisper. "Someone's trying to get in, captain."

"I'm not a captain anymore," he replied automatically, trying to clear the fog of sleep from his brain.

"You'll always be my captain, Erik. Now focus! Whoever is out there has been making noises for almost a minute now, so they're clearly not authorized to enter."

The words snapped him into wakefulness, the fear returning. "This could be how they get rid of us. Send a small group, toss us out of the airlock or smash our heads in, and claim it was payback for the fight and they couldn't identify the perpetrators."

Isaac moaned nearby at the words, but Fynn snapped back "It could also be a rescue attempt, Erik."

"Who'd want to rescue us on this cursed ship?" he asked morosely. A sharp, stinging slap jerked his head back and he turned to Fynn with anger burning in his eyes. A moment later he calmed and nodded his thanks. "Sorry, old friend, I got lost in myself for a while."

Erik climbed to his feet and stepped closer to the door, hearing the scratching and soft clicking sound of the security panel being forcibly removed. He returned to the others and spoke softly. "Whether this is friend or foe, we need to be ready. You two stand against the wall over there, and I'll wait by the door to jump them as they enter."

"Not the best plan, but it'll work. Come with me, Isaac." Fynn pulled the technician to the far wall and they waited there as Erik returned to the door. He tapped the switch to dim the lights in the cabin, and then placed his back against the bulkhead a few feet from where the door would open.

The wait was not long, as half a minute later the door slid aside and a low cry of victory was heard from the other side. A slight figure entered the darkened room, light from the corridor streaming in around them. The person paused long enough to spot Isaac and Fynn, raising a hand toward them. Erik acted quickly, not wanting to risk that hand holding a weapon, tackling the figure and wrapping his arms around his opponent to prevent movement.

"Whoa!" a voice called quietly from the doorway as a second person entered. "We're friends! None of us are armed." A third person entered behind, hands raised to show that they were empty, followed by a fourth and fifth person dragging two unconscious marines into the cabin. They dropped a few empty alcohol bottles by the sleeping troopers, then crouched by the portal to keep an eye on the corridor in both directions.

"What do you want with us?" Erik asked, holding tightly to the person he held wrapped in his arms. The first three intruders were dressed in Syndicate uniforms with no rank designations, the two crouching by the door in basic light marine armor.

The person with raised hands turned to let the light from the corridor reveal a man with a face that seemed familiar. Erik stared at him for a few moments, then cried out in surprise as the pieces fit together. He released the person who had been struggling against him, standing in shock. "My name is Altan Sansar," the revealed man announced. "I believe you know my sister, Tuya."

"What?" Isaac asked, as he and Fynn approached. "Her brother is dead."

"Supposed to be dead," Erik added, stepping forward with narrowed eyes. "The ship was destroyed but the crew weren't onboard, were they? Just as our ship will be damaged while we remain here on the *Indomitable*."

"That's correct." Altan lowered his hands, and gestured to the four others who'd entered with him. "This is everyone who survived from the crew of the *Telemachus*. I'll share our story, if you'll allow us to remain. I assure you that this cabin is not being monitored." Erik nodded and the two men in marine uniforms stepped out into the corridor to take the place of the guards. The door closed as they took up positions to either side of it.

"The two marines are Richard and Tom, who served as cargo haulers on the *Telemachus*," Altan said, then waved at the two who remained in the cabin. "The woman you were holding so tightly is Jen, our doctor. The last of us is Mira, pilot extraordinaire."

Jen stared daggers at Erik, tugging her uniform straight, then turned to nod curtly at Fynn and Isaac. She leaned against the wall near the door with her arms crossed. Mira smiled as she was introduced, and took a seat in one of the chairs as Altan sat in another. Erik and Fynn joined them, while Isaac retreated to sit on a bunk with eyes darting around at each of the newcomers.

"Tuya shared the story of your disappearance and assumed death with Fynn and Isaac just this morning," Erik said. "I only found out a few months ago at the start of this trip, when she recognized the cargo container as being the same that you described on your last guild job."

"She remembered my sparse details that well after half a decade? My biggest fear all these years has been that she would forget me, or give up her dreams because of what happened to me."

"Quite the opposite. She joined the *Vagabond* because she clung to her dream of following you into space even harder than before your loss. I think she may harbor secret hopes of finding out the truth, which unfortunately appears to have happened."

Altan leaned back and heaved a deep sigh. "I heard she was taken. My friends and I were working on plans to get in here as soon as we heard that another freighter crew had been taken prisoner, but it took us hours to find the guard schedules and to all be off shift at the same time. I hope to still see my sister again."

"Tuya is the toughest person I know, and if anyone can survive whatever they do it will be her."

Mira leaned forward with an inquisitive eyebrow raised. "Is it true she took on two marines at once?"

"And beat them!" Fynn said triumphantly. "Don't tussle with a person who has implants."

"Implants?" Altan asked in surprise. "When did she get those?"

Erik shrugged. "She had them when she joined our crew four years ago, but I never asked for details. With something that illegal, I knew she would bring it up if she ever wanted to talk about it."

"Sounds like my sister has been through some interesting times of her own."

"Speaking of which, will you tell us how most of the crew of a freighter ended up working on a secret Syndicate ship?"

Altan pursed his lips for a moment, and then replied. "To start with, the *Indomitable* is more than just a ship. I'm sure you saw the size of her, or you wouldn't have been taken prisoner. She is the first ship designated as a heavy cruiser by the Syndicate Navy. *Indomitable* was built to be an overwhelming force against the Coalition ships, heavily armed with twenty-four railgun emplacements, four forward torpedo launchers, and two rear torpedo launchers. She also carries a full squadron of twelve Dart class fighters and another squadron of armored personnel carriers for boarding enemy ships or ground assaults."

Fynn whistled in amazement. "That's more firepower than we estimated."

"As to how we became a part of the crew, that story starts with the captain of the *Telemachus* taking the same kind of job that led all of you here. The money was too good to pass up, of course, and it didn't help that we ran into issues on the previous run and barely walked away with any credits at all by the end of it. The constraints stipulated by the contract were extremely odd, but the money overruled all second thoughts."

"Sounds familiar," Erik added gloomily.

"I only told Tuya about how the container looked, but we actually carried three of them. They were so massive that they filled our cargo bay. A few people expressed doubts about making an eleven month round trip for a single job, but the objections were half-hearted at best.

"Once we were past the orbital path of Mars, control of the ship was turned over to our AI for the trip to the offload point and back to our starting point. The captain was upset by that more than any other restriction of the contract, because he'd never grown comfortable with a semi-sentient computer in control of any major part of his ship. Everything ran smoothly, though, and the crew were happy since we spent most of our days in our cabins or the rec room goofing off. A few of us missed being able to see the view outside the ship, but we were able to pull up recorded views from other trips and satisfy ourselves with those.

"As it turns out, all of that downtime is what led to the five of us ending up here. Our engineer and computer technician got bored, and started tinkering with the ship to see if they could bypass the AI controls enough to get a view of our destination when we arrived. It took them a few weeks, but they succeeded a day before we arrived at the *Indomitable*." Altan paused, and shrugged. "Well, they mostly succeeded. You see, the AI had detected the changed coding, and while it couldn't try to override the bypass it did log the action and forward it to the Syndicate AI with the hourly progress reports it was sending out."

"Progress reports?" Erik turned to look at Isaac, who shook his head to show he didn't know if Aurora had been sending similar reports before they shut down the AI.

"One of the stipulations in the contract," Altan explained. "It allows the Syndicate to keep track of the important shipments, and also provides clues when a crew is trying to circumvent the restrictions. Or when they break it, as both of our ships did. As soon as

Telemachus docked, the marines marched on board and took us all into custody."

He paused, and swallowed a lump in his throat. "Our captain protested and insisted that it was illegal for the Syndicate to take any action against us without notifying the guild and filing a grievance. The marines shot him. None of them even tried to calm him down, they just shot him and left him bleeding to death on the ship as they dragged the rest of us into the *Indomitable* and shoved the eight of us into a cabin just like this one.

"We languished there for half a year, with no contact other than a junior officer who would stop in once a week to ask us if we had any needs. Every visit, he would say that the admiral was deciding what to do with us, but we stopped expecting that decision fairly soon. He told us when the *Telemachus* was destroyed, and to give the boy credit he had sympathy in his voice. Not that it made us feel any better or more willing to be well disposed toward him."

Altan paused his story, rising to walk to the small kitchen and pour himself a cup of water. Sipping and returning to his chair, he continued.

"Finally, the admiral and his senior staff had made their decision. We were given an ultimatum: join the Syndicate navy and commit to years of serving aboard the *Indomitable* until construction and her first mission were complete, or die."

He shrugged. "We all accepted the offer to join them, but we never forgot the death of our captain or the imprisonment. As a group, we decided to become a part of the crew so that we would have opportunities to gather information and sabotage the construction as much as possible.

"It took more than a year, but we were finally accepted as part of the crew and the wariness around us all but disappeared. We had seen three other guild ships deliver shipments and then leave to accept their payments, and I confess that a small part of me had started to hate each of them for not suffering through the same things we had. The day after that third ship dropped off a couple of containers of computer cores and the first disassembled railgun, we met to discuss our first attempt at sabotage.

"*Indomitable* had spent years cruising through the asteroid belt, dispatching mining crews to pull out ores and minerals that could be used in her construction. The cargo containers brought in by guild freighters contained all the items that could not be constructed internally, which made them the most precious objects on the ship. So, we decided to destroy the most recent shipment and set the construction back by at least five or six months.

"Our plan went well. Half of the shipment was ejected from the ship to be destroyed in the vacuum while the other half was burned into uselessness by thermite charges. Unfortunately, three of our crew were caught in the process and charged with treason. Commander Guildersen was furious, and wanted the rest of us arrested and charged as well, but the admiral could find no proof that we had been involved. We were all demoted to the lowest ranks, never to receive promotion again, and were watched for a long while after having to see our friends executed as an example to the crew."

Jen let loose a muttered string of obscenities from her spot by the door, and Mira wiped away a tear. Altan reached over to place a reassuring hand over hers.

"We found opportunities for small bits of sabotage here and there after that, but never anything too significant. Jen finally got a job as an orderly in the med bay and Mira got posted to the bridge crew on the overnight shift. I ended up on one of the construction crews, while Tom and Richard were drafted into the marines as low-level grunts. When the *Indomitable* is complete and begins her mission, they'll be at the front lines and in the most danger."

"What's left to be completed?" Fynn asked with interest. "The construction looked finished when we were approaching to dock."

"The ship itself is operational," Altan said. "What's lacking is the weaponry and firepower, with only six functional railguns. The shipment you're carrying is two more railguns, a dozen torpedoes, and a crate of flechette rifles for the marines."

"Why wait until the final stages to install the weapons and stock the armory?" Erik asked incredulously.

"Because the ship has been running on a skeleton crew since construction began." Altan chuckled. "A skeleton of a skeleton crew, with there not being enough personnel for the minimal staffing levels. In order to hide the apparent disappearance of personnel, the Syndicate selects only unmarried candidates with no family ties so that few people question it if they stop hearing from them. On top of that, they can only deliver a dozen or so new crew and marines when a frigate happens to be passing through our approximate area. That only happens once or twice a year, at best. It's the reason they wanted us to join the crew."

"Then the crews of those frigates know about the *Indomitable*? Doesn't that reduce the secrecy?"

"Ah, Admiral Yumata is too smart for that," Altan replied with a smile. "He has the frigate drop the incoming personnel on an asteroid with temporary shelter and a month of rations and air. We wait nearby, cozied up to a rock large enough to hide us in its sensor shadow, and pick them up after a couple of days."

"The frigate crews assume that whatever posting the poor fools they've left behind are destined for is sending a ship, and is probably two or three weeks away and giving a bit of leeway on the amount of supplies." Erik sat back. He couldn't help but admire the effort being put into the project.

"Correct. The Syndicate started leaking reports of secret bases in the belt a year before construction on the *Indomitable* began. They became such common knowledge that everyone accepted them as poorly hidden fact the last time I was on Luna."

Fynn nodded. "It's still the same story. We all assumed this contract was delivery to one of those 'black sites', as everyone has taken to calling them."

Erik laughed bitterly. "In the last few years, assumptions have shifted from hidden mining colonies extracting valuable ores to stations set up as a jumping off point for exploration and eventual colonization of the outer system. Most people I've spoken with love the conspiracy theory that one or both Earth governments are setting up bases to retake control of the mining colonies."

Altan shared a glance with Mira. "The speculation when we left was much more nebulous. I'm surprised that perception came so very close to the truth."

"You mean the conspiracy theory was right?"

"Somewhat. The *Indomitable*'s mission, once she is complete and ready to be revealed, is to destroy the Coalition's part of the scientific teams on Mars before heading to Luna to obliterate Aldrin dome. The military committee feels confident that both tasks can be completed before the Coalition can assemble their small fleet of frigates to stop the advance."

Erik felt the blood drain from his face. "The guild headquarters are in Aldrin dome because they wouldn't let us have a presence in Armstrong. They'll kill thousands of people there, and several hundred more on Mars."

"Plus thousands more on all the frigates," Altan nodded. "And it won't stop there. The enmity between the two governments is too strong for the Coalition to surrender after those blows. The admiral's next task is targeted bombardment of military and government buildings in major Coalition cities, starting with London and Paris. They will also drop marines and special recon troopers into those cities."

"Millions," Fynn whispered. "Tens of millions, in each of those cities. All of them innocent and not knowing what's coming."

Erik clenched his fists, slamming them on the arms of his chair. "We have to do something to stop all this, or at the very least get a warning out."

Jen smiled mockingly at him. "How are you going to do that, hero? This ship is lightly crewed, but there are still five hundred naval crew and four marine squads."

He ran through the options mentally, his jaw clenching each time he concluded an idea wouldn't work. Minutes passed in silence, and he could feel the eyes of the old *Telemachus* crew on him. With a grimace, he decided that there were only two ideas he could see having even a small chance of success.

"How many people are on the bridge during shifts?"

Mira shook her head. "We considered that in our first year as part of the crew. The day shifts have six people on the bridge at all times, with another six that are in and out throughout. There are also three marines stationed at points on the bridge, to cover all entrances." She shrugged. "The overnight shift I work on has four people manning the bridge, still with three marines."

"What about getting Richard and Tom on that overnight watch? If they were on the bridge with you, it would be simple to subdue the remaining marine and lock down the other crew members."

"Won't work," Mira replied shortly. "They're both rank and file grunts, and bridge duty is reserved for officers or NCO's. They get the shit jobs that no one else wants to do and have no real responsibility."

Erik sighed. "I guess that idea is out, then. I liked it a lot better than my other one." He glanced around at each person in the room. "You need to get to our ship, and take it out of here. I can give you the command codes to unlock the systems, but with the state the *Vagabond* is in I don't know how far you will get before they catch you."

He leaned forward, and told of the events that had transpired on his ship since departing from Interamnia. Mira winced several times as he and Fynn detailed the hull damage caused by the hard acceleration burn and the steps they had to take to shut down the AI. Erik motioned Isaac forward to talk about how the ship's computer had been neglected and stripped down over the years as his advanced AI took over more and more functions, and to explain the limitations of the ship without that basic software now that everything was under manual control.

"So," Erik concluded, "you can see that the *Vagabond* is not capable of a quick getaway at the moment. And with our communications down, you couldn't even use her to send messages out to warn people."

"That wouldn't help, anyway," Altan responded. "The *Indomitable* has a jammer that extends several kilometers out from the ship. None of the crew are allowed to send or receive messages, but the admiral didn't trust everyone to be able to resist homesickness or the temptation to share a juicy secret with old friends."

"We're left with no options, then." Erik closed his eyes and felt the spiraling depression begin to descend upon him again.

"There is one," Isaac spoke quietly from the bunk he had retreated back to. "I'm not sure it's a good one." Everyone turned to look at him expectantly, and he blushed a deep crimson at the attention.

"What's your idea, Isaac?" Erik prompted.

"Well... Mira, how much access do you have to the computer via your terminal on the bridge?"

"I'm locked out of weapons systems and communications, but everything else I've had to work with has been open. The ship's AI monitors our activities, of course, but she only logs them and flags anything that would be considered outside of our scope."

"Have you done any work with the operating system, or would you have access to it?"

Her eyes widened as she understood what he was getting at. "There have been a few times I've needed to manipulate software to change functions or enable new ones as a part of the ship came online. So, I have access to it. And before you ask, I could create a copy of the operating system on a non-secure partition of the ship's server. Our AI would flag something like that, but since it could be explained as creating a backup before making changes it would be days before anyone checks up on the flag, if they ever do."

"That's great news. Altan, as part of the construction crew you can get outside the ship?"

"Half of my job is tethered work outside. We've been installing the railguns the last few months, and most of that is done outside the ship once the housing is in place and ready for the gun."

"Are you monitored closely?"

"Not as much as I was in the early days. Our shift supervisors have to oversee so many jobs that they check that we're actually outside the ship most of the time, and then check our work near the end of shift."

"Excellent." Isaac's face broke into a wide smile of delight. "The final piece is Jen. You have a terminal in the med bay that you have full access to?"

The doctor raised an indignant eyebrow. "They have me working as an orderly. Me, with my eight years of university and a full PHD and MD." A wicked smile spread across her face. "The ship's doctor and nurse are so fresh from university that they started letting me do most of the work after I spent a few months showing I was better at it then both of them. I have access to everything in medical."

Erik was unable to contain his own grin. "I see where this plan is going, and I like it."

"This just might work," Altan said, with an answering smile. "Let's hash out the details, and my team can start putting the wheels in motion."

An hour later, with the steps of the plan decided, Richard and Tom rejoined the group to drag the snoring door guards back into the corridor and drop the empty alcohol bottles in the middle of the corridor. All traces of the drug that had laced the booze was washed away, and they would waken with painful hangovers, too ashamed to confess the lapse in security to their superiors.

ELEVEN

Mira walked onto the bridge just as the chimes signaling the start of the graveyard shift sounded. She nodded to the marine guard at the door, moving sinuously between consoles to reach her station. Because of her skill from piloting a guild freighter for almost a decade, the ship's captain had recognized that she was one of the most experienced crew members on the bridge. Unfortunately, the inability to fully trust her loyalty had restricted her to the least desired shifts and limited the scope of work that was given to her.

This evening, she had a long list of tasks to work through. The logs from each of the day shifts needed to be examined to ensure that the ship's navigational system was still correctly calibrated. After that she needed to scan the commands executed by the AI; the semi-sentient machine intelligence was viewed with much more skepticism on military vessels than the independent freighters. She set to work on the logs right away.

It was well after midnight by the time the log review was completed, having taken nearly twice as long as usual. Her focus kept wandering, leaving her to reread entries multiple times before she processed the data in front of her. Mira marked a few of the logs for a deeper review by the navigational officer in the morning shift, and then crossed the task off her mental checklist.

Looking around at her few coworkers, noting with disdain that two of them appeared to be napping at their stations, she made sure that no one was paying her any special attention. Two of the marine guards could not see her terminal, and the one who could was currently lusting after the young ensign manning the command chair and could not take his eyes off of her.

Confident that she was unobserved, Mira casually typed at the terminal keypad to bring up the operating system's service menu. She created a partition on the public server, giving it a generic name that would draw no one's attention. A few more keystrokes and the computer was copying its root system over to the empty partition, showing only a progress bar on her screen.

Impatiently watching the bar fill toward completion, she pulled her tablet to sit in front of her and connected to the ship's logs on it. She scrolled through looking for specific keywords, and finally found a note filed by the security station an hour earlier that a prisoner had been interrogated and was being sent to medical for treatment before resuming. The only prisoner being held in the security section was Tuya, and she was relieved to see the addendum about the interrogation continuing since that meant nothing had been gleaned so far. She sent a quick coded message out to Altan.

Long minutes later, the progress bar was full and displaying a message that the copy was complete. Mira verified the integrity of the o/s files on the partition, buried it under several subdirectories, and closed out of the system's service menu. She breathed a sigh of relief, looking around the bridge once more.

Rising from her seat, she approached the ensign and requested the shift password to the AI's programming. Her voice seemed to quaver with nerves, but the ensign sent the password through to her terminal without any hesitation. Mira sent a brief prayer to the gods for the obliviousness of people stuck in a late night shift who feel their potential is not being served and therefore put in little effort.

She returned to her station and got logged on to the AI system structure. She perused the scans that she was tasked with reviewing for a while, and then nonchalantly pulled up the AI logs of her workstation. The operating system copy had been flagged as she suspected, but given a very low priority so that it blended in with the flags on all other work being done by the bridge crew. If anyone bothered to look at flags, it would be almost impossible for them to pick out that single item as a concern to follow up on.

Mira smiled in relief that her part of the plan was complete, and settled in to complete normal work for the rest of her shift.

TWELVE

After the meeting between the two freighter crews had broken up, Erik and his two remaining friends were able to push aside racing thoughts and worry for Tuya long enough to get a few hours of sleep. When the clock showed the time as six in the morning, the three of them were refreshed and showered.

The door opened to reveal two new marine guards, with a third pushing in a small cart of food supplies for the cabin. Tom tossed a wink at the *Vagabond* crew, growling at them to remain on the other side of the cabin as he unloaded a few boxes of protein bars and powdered meal packs. He discreetly patted the second box off the cart a few times before continuing to unload, and then rolled the cart out of the room without a backwards glance.

Once the doors were closed, Erik hurried over to shove the boxes aside until he found the indicated box. He ripped the strip of tape off, and flipped aside the flaps to reveal stacks of protein bars. Pulling them out one by one, he finally revealed a small slip of paper stuck in the middle of the stacks. *Tuya transferred to medical early a.m.,* the note read. *Minor injuries, still silent, ship safe and load secure.*

The three friends shared smiles. Erik felt a heavy weight lift from his shoulders that he had not even realized was there, and felt a burst of optimism that their plans would work out. Leaving the unopened boxes, they each nibbled at a protein bar to make sure they had the energy they would need for the day's events.

Sitting in nervous tension, each man was running through scenarios over and over to try and prepare for any eventuality. The clock chimed to signify the shift change at seven, and Erik rose with a deep sigh.

"Is everyone ready?"

Fynn and Isaac nodded, the engineer resolute while the technician was a bundle of nerves. Erik twisted his head to try and relieve muscles sore from a stressful night, and finally waved Isaac forward.

"I apologize again for this."

"It's okay, captain. The mission requires it, and so do the lives of millions."

Erik grabbed the man's left hand and gripped his upper arm, holding it steady as Fynn stepped forward with the metal leg from one of the bunks they had managed to loosen the bolts on overnight. He swung the thin rod up and then brought it down as hard as he could on the midpoint of Isaac's forearm. A loud snap echoed through the cabin, and Isaac cried out with the shock of the blow.

"It doesn't hurt," he said in amazement, staring down at the sleeve of his jumpsuit that showed a prominent bulge where the broken bone was pushing up against skin.

"The pain will come," Erik told him. "As soon as the shock and adrenaline wear off. That usually doesn't take long, so I'd expect..."

He broke off as Isaac cried out once more as the pain began to hit. The tech cradled his injured arm against his chest, face going white and sweat breaking out across his brow. Fynn swung the metal bunk leg around the cabin to smash against the walls and make as much noise as possible, making it look like a furious fight had erupted.

Erik hurried to the cabin door and started banging against it with one of the room's chairs. He slammed the chair against the metal door repeatedly, yelling that they needed medical help. The chair was breaking into pieces and he was about to grab a second, when the door slid open and the two marines burst into the room with weapons drawn.

"Get down on the ground!" the first trooper yelled at Erik, as the second marine shifted to cover the other two men.

"My friends got into a fight, and Isaac hurt his arm," Erik called out as he dropped to his knees and then lay face down with his hands extended. "You have to get him to the med bay."

Isaac was still staring down at his broken arm with wide eyes, whimpering at the pain racing through his body. Fynn dropped his impromptu weapon and lay on the floor, calling out that he would do worse if Isaac didn't shut his filthy mouth and glaring at the technician across the room. The second marine roughly pushed the sleeve of Isaac's jumpsuit back, eliciting a yelp of pain and revealing a dark purple bruise spreading out from the location of the break.

The marines traded cynical glances. "We could leave him," the first suggested. "Let the next shift deal with the paperwork."

"Please!" Erik pleaded. "You can't leave him like that for hours. The pain is already unbearable, and if that arm isn't set it could never be right again."

"Not sure that will matter much," the second marine chuckled nastily. He finally shrugged and pulled Isaac around to escort him from the cabin, calling in for a medical transport at their location. The first marine backed out of the room with his weapon sliding between the two prone men. He stopped near the shattered chair long enough to stare daggers at the two men on the floor. "You might need to visit medical yourself when our sergeant sees the damage you caused."

THIRTEEN

Isaac had lived a sheltered childhood, always a loner who was happiest in a dark corner reading books or playing games on his tablet. During his university years, he retreated to his dorm room between classes to code programs and work out algorithms to improve functions. After joining the crew of the *Vagabond* to maintain the computer systems and the AI, he was rarely found outside the technical room.

All of which meant that he had never broken a bone before and had less experience with pain than most people in their middle age. He knew he was not handling this experience well, but the pain pulsing through his arm made him forget any resolve to fight through it. He could feel that he was being propelled down the corridors, but couldn't focus on anything long enough to know where he was or which direction they were heading.

When he was pushed down onto a hard plastic bed, he regained enough awareness to register the clean white surfaces and antiseptic smell of a medical bay. He knew he should be happy to be there, that it meant the plan was working so far, but his thoughts soon scattered into the haze of pain. He was aware of voices around him, had the sense they were asking him questions he couldn't understand, and then felt a sharp jab in the shoulder of the broken arm.

The pain faded slowly, replaced by a dull ache accompanied by a lightness that made Isaac feel as if he were floating above the bed. He worked to focus his eyes, and smiled to see Jen standing above him in the teal uniform of the medical staff. Her mouth was moving but it took a few moments for the words to be processed by his brain.

"I need to set the bone, sir," she enunciated loudly. "You will feel a tug. Don't fight it."

"You're pretty," Isaac said through a dopey smile as she disappeared from his view. He turned his head to look around the room, seeing a blank terminal screen nearby which created a niggling thought that he couldn't seem to capture. Someone picked up his hand as he stared at the screen, trying to remember why it seemed important, and then he felt a sharp jerk followed by a wave of pain that cut through the morphine. He cried out and jerked his head around to see Jen placing a rigid splint around his arm, covering it from his elbow to his wrist and wrapping around his thumb.

"Ow, Jen," he complained quietly.

"I'm sorry for the pain, *sir*," she said, emphasizing the last word and squinting her eyes at him. "The morphine will help to minimize it for now, and the doctor will be by in a few hours to take a closer look at your bone and make sure we don't need to go in and surgically repair anything."

"Oh," Isaac said, reddening at his mistake. "Uh, thank you, ma'am. Nurse? Ma'am."

"I'll pull the privacy curtain so that you can rest," Jen told him, glancing up to make sure that no one was looking in their direction before jabbing him with another needle quickly. "The morphine will cause drowsiness, and sleep is the best way for our bodies to repair themselves." She leaned down, the corners of her mouth curling up. "And thank you for the compliment, handsome." With a gentle pat on his shoulder, she reached up to slide a thin curtain around the bed to hide him from the rest of the room, and then walked away.

Isaac felt a burst of energy through his body from the second injection. Against all his expectations, the pain faded to an even duller ache as the stimulant and morphine mixed in his system. After a few moments to adjust to the drugs coursing through his veins, he swung his legs off the bed and stumbled over to sit in the rolling chair in front of the terminal. He glanced at the curtain to make sure he could not be seen in his new position. Assured of privacy he flicked the button to turn on the screen.

Jen had left the terminal signed on to the system, which allowed him to access the system directory and find the public server partition where Mira had stored a copy of the *Indomitable*'s operating system. Isaac looked through the software and pulled up sections of code to compare it to his memory of a guild freighter's standard o/s. There were many similarities, but more inconsistencies than he would normally be comfortable with. Luckily, the most important software that controlled most of the engine room and bridge was functionally similar to what *Vagabond* had worked with. Working as quickly as he could with one hand partially immobilized, he sifted through the programs, walling off anything that would not be needed on the freighter so as to keep them from bogging down the limited processors. Compared to the power of a system on a military ship, the freighter's computer was pitifully weak and could not handle running so much concurrent software.

He checked the clock after what felt like minutes and found that he had spent nearly an hour working on the operating system files. To be safe, he needed to be off the terminal and back in the bed in no more than thirty minutes, in case the doctor or nurse checked in unexpectedly and Jen was unable to provide a warning. Moving quickly, he found the programming for the communication clusters on the military vessel. He pared that down to work with only the three antenna arrays on the *Vagabond*'s hull, and set the rest of the communications software to stay in sleep mode. Any messages sent from the freighter would appear as an anonymous sender until he could reload their specific communication protocols, but at least they could send and receive.

Confident that he had trimmed down the software enough to allow essential functions, Isaac keyed in the commands to send the operating system into another partition on the ship's server with security set to require a password to gain access. As he did so, the main doors hissed open and Isaac could hear footsteps approach his curtained-off area. A male voice called out a greeting, returned by another voice muffled by distance. Isaac closed a few open windows on the terminal screen, but knew he didn't have time to completely log off the system.

Quickly crawling back onto the rough plastic mattress his heart was beating fast. The stimulant racing through his system was fueling nothing but panic now. The glare of the terminal screen seemed to light the entire room, and Isaac realized he had forgotten to switch the screen off. He couldn't fight the feeling that whoever looked at him would see the guilt written across his transparent face.

The panic and fear were so overwhelming that he yelped in surprise when the curtain was thrust back and a young man in a doctor's coat entered. His head was down, reading from a tablet, and Isaac took the moment of freedom to try and compose himself.

"Mr. Szymanski? Do I have that right?" the doctor asked, looking up at last.

"Yes!" Isaac blurted shrilly, trying to sound normal and keep his eyes from darting to the terminal screen. "Yes, that's me. I'm Mr. Szymanski. Call me Isaac."

"Hmmm, very well." The doctor's eyes moved back to the tablet. "It looks like a standard oblique fracture of the radius. Not bad enough to use nanos to do a repair, thankfully, since our supply of that is low." The doctor smiled up at Isaac, as if expecting him to be glad to not cause the use of the important nanobots.

"Anyway," the doctor continued with a frown when he got no response but confused wide eyes. "I'll have the orderly inject a fluid that will do a basic re-knitting of the bone so that we have a jump on the healing. You'll still have to wear a hard cast for a few weeks, but should have full mobility."

"Um, thanks?" Isaac couldn't believe the man hadn't seen through him and called for the marines standing at the exit to the med bay. The doctor walked away without another word, tapping on the tablet to make notes. One of the marines glanced over briefly, but his bored expression never altered and he faced forward again after assuring himself that the prisoner was still in the same spot.

Ten minutes later, Jen returned and pulled the curtain to halfway block the view of the area. Her eyes darted to the lit screen and she detoured to turn off the terminal. She then removed the splint and placed an autoinjector against his wrist, pressing the trigger to slowly inject a milky white fluid that made Isaac's arm tingle and go cold.

"It's done?" she asked quietly, remaining focused on her task.

"Mmhmm," Isaac murmured, not enjoying the sensation of the viscous liquid flowing through his forearm. He imagined he could feel the fluid wrapping around his bones and absorbing into the structure, to bridge the break and begin the process of fusing the two pieces back into one. Objectively, he knew the process would take half a day or more to work.

"I'll send the signal to Altan," Jen muttered, then pulled the autoinjector away and looked up to speak in her normal brisk tone to the nearby marines. "Mr. Szymanski will need to remain in medical for a few hours so we can monitor and make sure the fluid is working properly."

She stepped across the space to place the device on a tray of used equipment that would be sterilized, and returned to his bedside to put the splint back on his arm. "Tuya is in the bed directly across from you," she whispered. "It looks like she took a beating, but she'll be released later today with nothing more than a dozen stitches and few yards of dressing."

Isaac nodded gratefully, relaxing and closing his eyes. His part of the plan was complete for now, and he could rest easy knowing it had been successful.

FOURTEEN

Altan had walked the corridor past the medical bay several times in the early morning hours, resisting an urge to manufacture a reason to go inside and see his sister. It was still hard for him to believe that she was on the same ship after so many years apart, and yet it felt as if the distance between them had never been greater. How would she react if she saw a brother she thought long dead? Would he see disgust in her eyes when she saw the Syndicate uniform he still despised putting on every day?

The crew of the *Telemachus* had grown so accustomed to their situation that none of them thought of the system outside of the Syndicate ship very often anymore. A twinge of guilt or disgust would rear up when some officer or crew member made a joke about destroying the Mars outpost or two thirds of the Luna population, but long acclimatization had stopped the urges to speak up against the planned mission. The five of them still resisted whenever they could, but that had become empty gestures such as disconnecting one small wire while working to fix another or leaving a rivet out when attaching a hull plate. The inconvenience was minor, if it was ever noticed at all, and easily fixed.

Every time a guild ship had dropped off shipments for the *Indomitable*, the five of them had felt the faint stirring of their old rebellious fire. Each time they hoped the crew of the ship had followed directives and would be allowed to leave, and yet they also hoped the crew would be taken into custody to join them in the Syndicate crew as more people to sympathize with.

When the *Vagabond* had flown past in such dramatic fashion, and stirred the ship into a panic that their secret would be exposed, it had fueled those fires into an all-consuming blaze. Even Richard, who had begun to act as if he was happier with marine discipline than his previous freedom, was instantly alert to the possibilities presented by the event. The five old crewmates had held long sessions during the week it took for the *Vagabond* to make the return trip, discussing options for disabling the *Indomitable* and making a dramatic escape with the unknown crew of the guild ship.

Finding out that his sister was aboard that vessel had come as such a shock to Altan that he had almost run to the lieutenant commander in charge of the construction crews to beg an opportunity to see her, willing to offer up his friends and the plans they had all discussed together. He was ashamed of how close he had come to giving in to that impulse, ashamed that he could harbor such disloyalty to friends he had known for a decade.

Now, having met the *Vagabond*'s crew, he was doubly glad that he had resisted the impulse. The three men had exuded a competence and independent spirit that called out to him, raising his hopes and optimism. He felt closer to freedom than he had since those long ago days before he had to watch three of his friends die at the hands of men and women he now had to work with.

His reverie was interrupted by a soft vibration in his jacket's inner pocket. He pulled out the small tablet and smiled to see the message from Jen confirming completion of Isaac's part of the plan. Altan slid the tablet back into his pocket, took a deep breath to steady his nerves, and marched through the corridors into the construction team's locker room.

"Hey, Alt!" a woman called from across the room, where she was pulling on a jumpsuit. "You're early today."

"Josie," he responded. "Couldn't sleep last night, and I'm getting bored wandering the ship. Thought I'd get a jump on all the work today, and maybe the supervisor won't ride my ass as much as usual."

The woman laughed, nodding in agreement. "Just be glad you weren't working the early morning shift with my team. Those lug head marines were swarming all over that freighter, getting in the way every time we needed to be working in that area. I had to put in an extra hour because they slowed me down so much."

Altan groaned in sympathy. The construction and maintenance crews were always fighting with the marine commanders over who had precedence during EVA; C&M maintained that keeping the ship functional was most important, while the marine command insisted that training maneuvers were a higher priority.

"I'll keep an eye out for them. I think my group is checking the hull plating on that side of the ship today."

"Oh, you won't have to worry. The marines all got recalled into the ship a few hours ago. It looks like they gave up on trying to crack the freighter open for now."

He had to fight to keep an exultant grin from his face and maintain an expression that showed he didn't care what the marines were doing as long as they weren't in the way. "In that case, maybe I can finish quick and knock off early today."

Josie laughed loudly. "The day they let anyone end a shift early will be the day they promote me to admiral."

"Yeah, but a guy can dream." Altan said wistfully, storing his jacket and boots in the locker and waving as the woman left the locker room. He quickly shucked off the jumpsuit and shimmied into the skintight bio suit that was worn under the EVA suits. With a glance around to confirm he was still alone, he grabbed his tablet and shoved it into a zippered compartment over his chest.

Walking through a door at the opposite end of the locker room, he entered the airlock antechamber. The walls were lined with yellow and red EVA suits; yellow denoted a crew doing construction, and red denoted workers performing maintenance duties. Altan grabbed a red suit and laboriously stuffed himself into the bulky confines. He shifted the tablet around to an arm pouch of the exterior suit, making sure the surface was ready for use but not easily visible. Carrying the device outside the ship was prohibited and would earn him a few days in a cell if he were caught.

He pulled a helmet from a shelf, and twisted it onto the collar at his neck. Snapping down a few latches locked the helmet in place, and the holographic HUD flickered into existence. A quick check verified the suit integrity, showed his oxygen and nitrogen reserves were near a hundred percent, and that he had clearance to leave the ship.

Altan pressed on the panel near the airlock to signal his desire to enter, and waited a few seconds as the ship's computer verified the chamber was empty and pressurized before the doors cycled open. As soon as he was inside, the doors closed again and he waited as the air was sucked from the chamber. The red light over the exterior portal flicked to green, and he watched as the hatch irised open.

The view of the star field with a handful of asteroids near enough to look like small moons was breathtaking no matter how many times he experienced it. This side of the ship looked toward the outer system, and on the rare occasions that the orbits were right he could marvel at Saturn or Jupiter looming large.

He attached his tether to the rail just outside the airlock, part of a system that ran all over the ship and allowed crews and marines to safely traverse the vast bulk. Engaging the mag boots, he stepped out and felt his stomach shift as his orientation changed and his brain took a second to adjust. The first couple of dozen times he had walked the skin of a ship had left him nauseous and fighting to not puke his guts up in the helmet, but the feeling barely registered now that he had years of experience. The airlock hatch hissed behind him as it closed, and he automatically took a handful of steps forward to be clear in case it would disgorge another worker soon after.

The clock in the corner of his HUD showed that he had over an hour before his normal shift started, and he knew his supervisor would not check in to see what he was working on until the entire crew was outside the ship. Stepping as quickly as the mag boots allowed, he began the long journey under the belly of the *Indomitable* and around to the hatch where the freighter was docked. Occasionally, he would release the magnetic hold of the boots and push himself forward to float quickly along a rail with his tether, engaging the boots again just long enough to switch over to a new rail when he reached a junction.

A long half hour later, Altan finally saw the *Vagabond* rising like the sun over the horizon of the ship ahead of him. The curve of the ship's belly was slight, but it so dwarfed a human figure that it felt like climbing up and then down a mountain. He paused once the freighter was fully in view, checking to be sure that the marine squad had not returned to resume their brute force attempt to enter the vessel. Finding the area uninhabited, he continued his gliding sprint and reached the docking tunnel.

Now came the most difficult and dangerous part of the operation, as he had to unclip his tether and push himself along the flexible docking tube. He was breathing heavily with exertion and concern, sweat beading his brow despite the air flow within the suit trying to keep condensation levels down.

Altan made the mistake of looking "up" at the star field between the two ships, and almost missed his next handhold as vertigo began to take hold. He squeezed his eyes shut, held himself in place until the panic was under control, and then started moving with shorter pushes to give him more contact with the tube.

Upon reaching the freighter, he gratefully engaged the mag boots and secured himself to the scuffed metal hull plating. With the time advancing swiftly, he could pause only a few seconds to catch his breath before beginning clunking steps along the ship. Erik had described the area around the maintenance hatch that allowed someone to manually exit the ship if the airlock was broken. Altan swept his eyes across the pocked and scarred surface of the freighter, looking for anything that matched. A hundred or so steps later, he finally spotted the bright shine of a repair weld that was only a year old, and followed the directions to find a second landmark. He saw the faint outline of the maintenance hatch, and pushed a panel forward to reveal the crank that would pop the hatch.

Placing his feet wide and engaging the magnetics at their highest level to provide leverage, Altan grabbed the wheel and strained to turn it. It refused to move at all, and he began to fear that the mechanism had frozen up from lack of use.

He took a deep breath, reset his grip, and pulled on the wheel with every bit of strength he could muster. One of his boots shifted as the force caused him to push hard against that foot, but it grabbed hold again and remained steady. Finally, the wheel jerked and began to move slowly through a half circle. The maintenance hatch popped up a few inches, and he could feel air flooding out into the vacuum around his ankles.

He grabbed the lip of the hatch, heaving it up on little-used hinges to reveal a small compartment that was barely large enough for an average person to fit into with an EVA suit on. Folding himself as much as the thick suit allowed, he shoved into the opening and then pulled the hatch closed behind him, turning the wheel on the bottom to lock it into position.

The compartment was lit only by the faint glow of his helmet's lights, and he searched for the panel he knew would be there. Once he found it, he had to squirm around to get a better angle so that he could press the button to activate it. A prompt appeared asking for a security code. He typed in the string of numbers and letters that Erik had given him the evening before.

Altan was rewarded with a burst of air as the compartment was pressurized, and then a section of the floor began to tilt down and dumped him into the corridor outside the engine room. Climbing to his feet, he removed his helmet and set it down against the bulkhead while he looked around to get his bearings. He hurried through the corridor, seeing a row of cabins on the interior and looking into the rec room and galley as he passed them by. Entering the control center, he pulled at the straps on his left hand to free his fingers. Without the bulk of the EVA suit glove, he keyed in the security code on the terminal near the command chair. The code was accepted, and the limited systems of the freighter came to life.

There were only fifteen minutes left, and he tapped at the terminal to execute the commands Isaac had gone over with him several times to be sure he had them memorized. The docking tube from *Indomitable* included a connection with the cruiser's computer, allowing him to access the server partition using Isaac's password. A few keystrokes later, the operating system was downloading into the *Vagabond*'s memory cores. Altan watched nervously as the progress bar ticked across the screen. Once the download was complete, he disconnected the freighter from the military ship's systems and entered the short command line that would execute the code to install the new operating system on the computer.

Altan raced back down the corridor, reattaching his suit's glove and then the helmet as he reached the maintenance hatch. He jumped up to grab the short ladder on the open compartment and pulled himself up, pressing the button to close the panel below him and then depressurize the space.

Barely waiting for the process to complete, he turned the wheel to pop open the outer hatch and pulled himself out onto the hull. He swiftly closed and locked the hatch down again, keying in the final letters of the security password when his suit's radio crackled.

"Sansar! Where are you?" a faint voice called out. With the normal communications jammed in the area around the *Indomitable*, the suits used a focused beam radio that required line of sight. His supervisor and the work crew he belonged to were already rounding the belly of the massive warship and approaching the site they would be working at.

"Uh, thought I saw a bit of bubbling on one of the hull plates around the number seven railgun emplacement," Altan responded, rising to his feet and judging the distances and time he had left. "Heading back to the docking ring with that freighter now."

He didn't have time to retreat down the tunnel the way he had approached the guild ship. The only option open to him made the adrenaline surge through his body, as he looked across the hundred meter gap between the freighter and Syndicate ship. He flexed his legs, and hunkered down as much as the bulky EVA suit allowed.

With a deep breath, he pushed up with all his strength, releasing the hold of the mag boots at just the right moment to allow him to shoot across the gap between the ships. Altan held his breath unconsciously, knowing that the slightest bit of air escaping his suit could change his trajectory and send him shooting off into open space.

As the hull of the *Indomitable* grew closer, he jerked his torso forward to try and flip his legs around to land feet first. The erratic movement started his body spinning and he could feel the vertigo of seeing the two ships orbiting around him. Altan fought against the desire to close his eyes, afraid that he could miss the landing.

He impacted hip first, bouncing against the hull and starting to drift away. He waved his legs around in panic, one mag boot hitting the hull just enough to create a seal and cause his drifting body to swing into an upright position. The first foot clicked down and his second foot soon followed, securely attaching him to the hull plate.

Altan fought down the panic and adrenaline-fueled shakes, breathing deeply to calm himself. He reached out to snap his tether to a nearby rail, straightening up just as his work crew appeared around the edge of the docking tube.

"What the hell's going on, Sansar?" the supervisor yelled. "Your bio suit is reading all kinds of erratic heart rates and blood pressure."

"I just wanted to beat you guys here, boss," Altan replied weakly. "I think that may have been the fastest tether glide I've ever done."

"Well, no one's giving out brownie points for being a daredevil." The stocky woman set down the cold-welding rig so that it clamped onto the hull. "Everyone get to work!"

Altan smiled, turning his head to look at the battered freighter from the corner of his eye. The plan was working as they had hoped, so far, and the ship's systems should be booting up to full functionality within a few hours.

FIFTEEN

Isaac was returned to the cabin shortly after noon, the doctor having released him after another cursory examination. The marines who escorted him in were more gentle than the pair who carried him away, but Erik could still see the resentment in their eyes at having to do a job that they felt was beneath their training. He and Fynn helped the tech into a bunk, and crowded around to hear how things had gone in the medical bay.

"Did you get a chance to see her?" Erik asked when Isaac passed on the information Jen had given him about Tuya's condition.

"I got a brief glimpse of her when they were taking me out, but it looked like she was sleeping."

"Building up her strength for the next round of interrogation, no doubt," Fynn spat out angrily. "The longer she holds out, the more desperate they are going to get for answers and the rougher the questioning will be."

Erik put a consoling hand on the engineer's shoulder. "If Altan was able to get his part of the plan done, we should be moving into the next phase this afternoon."

"The most dangerous part of it, Erik. A part where Isaac and I are going to be more hindrance than help."

"No one else will see it that way, Fynn. I promise you that. Your parts may be small, but they are the most important and without them the plan itself could never work."

"Speaking of work," Isaac interjected. "This bone knitting stuff is still working away, and I can't believe how much of my energy is being used up. I'm going to get some sleep while I can."

"Of course, get rested up." Erik patted him reassuringly, and then retreated to the sitting area with Fynn.

They sat in silence for a while, lost in thought until they heard soft snores from the bunk. Erik leaned close, keeping his voice low so as not to disturb Isaac. "I know this is the kind of work you've never wanted to do, Fynn. I never wanted to be put into a position to make you do it, but it's vital now that this gets done so we can try to avert countless deaths."

"That's the thought that keeps me going and gives me the strength I'm going to need to get through this. I just don't know how I'm going to feel when this is done. If we survive it, that is."

"We'll make it through. We have good people working with us, we have a solid plan, and I can't help but feel that fate is helping guide us through this."

"Fate?" The engineer snorted a laugh. "I don't know that I ever much believed in the stuff, but I'll happily take whatever help it can throw our way for the next few hours." He paused, took a breath, and continued. "When we get off this monstrosity and back to Luna, we are all going to have a lot of soul searching to do."

"We are," Erik agreed. "But I have a feeling that the system will change around us after this, and we may have to change ourselves to fit in to the new normal."

"You've hit on my biggest fear, captain. I don't think I want to have to change to fit in to what I feel coming."

They sat in silence, trying to digest the uncomfortable future they each saw stretching out ahead of them. No matter how Erik projected the short-term future to work out, he couldn't see a path that didn't end in system-wide aggression and war. The guild freighters would have to change, as well, to survive in that new reality.

Sixteen

Tom made a last stroke with his razor, turning his face in the mirror to make sure he didn't miss a spot. Washing the foam from his face, he watched in the mirror as Richard flirted with a young woman who had joined their squad four months earlier, during the last drop of new crew members. He often worried that his friend was becoming too comfortable in their roles on the ship, but the effort being put into his performance today was entirely in service to the plan they had hatched the evening before.

A tinkling laugh and playful arm slap signaled success, and Tom smiled at his reflection before turning to walk across to his locker. He opened the latch and pulled a fresh bio suit out. Tossing his towel on the bench after patting his face dry a final time, he felt the young trooper brush by him on the way to the showers to clean up after her shift. He and Richard were alone in this part of the locker room.

"That looked like it went well," he said nonchalantly.

Richard gave him a roguish grin and wink. "I have yet to meet the young lady that can resist my charms."

Tom turned a horrified look on his friend. "You've only met five women in the entire system?"

"Ha. Ha. Ha." Richard threw up a middle finger in his direction. "Your mom kept me so busy I just didn't have time to get out much."

"Jerk," Tom laughed. "It's set then?"

"Yep, she's going to meet me in the appointed storage room at fourteen hundred for a happy little snog fest."

"I don't know if she'll be disappointed or overjoyed at what greets her."

"Disappointed, of course! Absolutely heartbroken, and she will spend the rest of her days wondering just how great it could have been."

"Oh, I'm sure she'll be wondering, but I think it will be more questioning why she ever thought a make out session with you was a good idea at all."

Richard zipped up the last section of his ash gray suit, closing the locker door and turning to walk out of the room. "You're just jealous because you know you had no shot at all with her."

"Yes, please teach me your wisdom, great one!" Tom called loudly, dropping to his knees and clasping his hands together in a begging posture. Richard held up both hands with the middle fingers outstretched as he left the room.

Tom rose to his feet and finished stuffing himself into his bio suit. He pulled from his locker the only memento he had left from the *Telemachus,* and shoved it into a pocket. He left the locker room, walking into the armory where he signed out a suit of light armor plating. Strapping on the pieces of rigid armor that would protect his torso and limbs, he glanced around the room at the seven other members of his squad as they readied for their shift. The three who had been selected for duty on the bridge were issued heavier armor and carried lethal flechette pistols, while the rest of the squad wore the same light armor that he did and would all carry stun pistols and collapsible batons.

Once he was fully equipped, he found Richard and they reported to the squad sergeant to start their shift. Because they were still seen as outsiders by the insular marines who had gone through a year of training on Earth, they were often posted together for jobs that were less desirable. Today they were assigned to patrol the corridors around the engineering and science sections that were on the lower levels of the ship.

The two continued trading barbs as they took a lift down through the ship to their assigned starting point. They were laughing together as they approached the pair of trooopers.

"It's about time you guys arrived," one of them complained.

"Calm down, buddy," Tom told him. "We're right on time, as always."

"Yeah, well, this is the kind of shit duty that low rates like you two should be doing, not decent marines like us who deserve better postings."

Richard grabbed at his chest over his heart. "You have cut me to the quick with your words, sir. I am not worthy of even your scorn."

The marine muttered as he and his partner pushed past to leave for the locker room. With lightning speed, Tom pulled the memento from where he had slipped it into his sleeve, and grabbed at the nearest trooper to turn the man around. The piece of metal in his hand, a torn and twisted scrap of the ship he had loved living on, was jammed up into the man's neck where the armor left a gap between plating and helmet. The marine grabbed at the embedded metal, staring at Tom with wide eyes as blood spurted between his fingers and he dropped to the floor of the corridor.

Richard acted at the same moment, pulling his baton and swinging it out to extend it before sweeping the second trooper off his feet. He leaped forward, landing with one knee on the man's chest and swinging the butt of the baton repeatedly into his face, cracking the visor. The weapon was soon covered in blood and bits of bone, but he kept hitting the man well after he was clearly dead.

Tom pulled his friend off the marine, raising his hands in defense when it looked like Richard might lash out at him. The spark of anger in his eyes slowly faded away, though, and they stood over the bodies breathing hard from the exertion. With a grunt of satisfaction, Richard bent and started to unstrap the armor pieces from the man he had killed. Tom watched for a moment, and then followed suit with the other marine. Soon, they had two sets of armor piled in the corridor and were peeling the bio suits off the men. One of the suits had bits of blood staining it around the neck, but it would be hard to spot once the blood was dry and the armor was covering most of the stains.

"What do we do with the bodies?" Tom asked, standing over them. Richard shrugged and motioned down the corridor in the opposite direction from which they had approached. The nuclear reactor was in that direction, with massive turbines and pools of water to cool the super-heated cores that created the energy the ship needed. It was not an easy task, but they dragged the corpses and disposed of them as quickly as possible.

Returning to the spot to grab up the salvaged armor and weapons, Tom checked the time on the small terminal built into the armor plating on the underside of his left forearm. "You need to get moving to your rendezvous, Romeo."

Richard grimaced, but nodded. "You okay getting all of this stuff to the staging point?"

"I'll get it done as quickly as I can. Just make sure you're there to meet me in time for the next stage."

"If I'm not there by fourteen thirty, then you know I screwed up somehow and it's time to abort."

The two old friends clasped hands quickly, and Tom watched Richard hurry away at a trot. He stacked all the armor into an unwieldy pile, with the bio suits in between to minimize the noise of the pieces rubbing together, and put the weapons on top. He could barely see over the top of the stack as he carried it unsteadily down the corridor, praying and hoping that a scientist or engineer wouldn't pick that moment to be walking around at a time when there was usually very little traffic.

Luck was with him, and he made it through half a mile of corridors and up two levels in a lift to reach an empty cabin a little later than he planned. He sorted the material into two separate piles again, and then settled in to wait for his partner to arrive.

The silence in the empty space became more and more oppressive as the clock continued to advance. The nerves were churning his stomach as the deadline hit and Richard had not appeared. He tried to come up with reasons that his partner would be late. Though he conjured up dozens of possibilities none of them made him feel safer or less worried. He resolved to give it another ten minutes before sending the abort signal to his co-conspirators.

Tom was tapping at his wrist tablet, keying in the message to signal failure, when the cabin door slid open and Richard fell into the room breathing hard from the exertion of racing through the corridors.

"Where the hell have you been? I was just about to send the abort signal!"

"Sorry, sorry. The girl grabbed me and put me in a lip lock as soon as I entered the room, and I enjoyed it too much to stop it right away."

"The entire plan was almost ruined because you were too horny to follow your part?" Tom felt anger warring with the relief that had bloomed on seeing his friend.

"It's not like that, I just kissed her for a short while. But I got control of myself and administered the sedative. On the way here I had to divert a few times to get around groups in the corridors, that's all."

He could tell that Richard was leaving something out, but assumed from long experience that the carnal encounter had been the real cause for the delay. He decided to let it drop for now, since they were already behind.

"We need to get moving. We're fifteen minutes behind schedule now."

"Speaking of which," Richard said, finally catching his breath. "Thank you for giving me a bit of leeway. I promise I'll be much better at arriving on time in the future."

"You were able to get the things we needed with her thumbprint access, right?" Richard nodded and patted his pocket to show the items were there. "Good. One last thing to do and then we can finally execute the plan."

SEVENTEEN

Tuya woke to find her body was still sending complaints of pain and soreness from all over. The marines who had "questioned" her during the night had been well trained to cause maximum damage with minimal outward signs, and there had been few parts of her body that they didn't touch.

She had been drifting in and out of consciousness as they dragged her to the med bay, but had caught enough of the conversations to understand that they were going to have her implants removed that afternoon so that she was unable to withstand so much pain. The thought of the removal hurt her more than any of the beatings. The main reason the cybernetic implants were illegal was because the body became dependent on them over time, and once they were removed it was incredibly likely that she would be left paralyzed or close to it.

She blinked her eyes open, the harsh light of the stark white chamber painful as her eyes adjusted. She could hear movement outside the curtain that walled her off from the rest of the large room, and lay silently listening. There was only one person moving around, but she had no doubt the ubiquitous marine guards were by the door watching carefully to ensure she did not try to escape. There had been discussion of shackling her to the bed, but they decided on heavy sedation instead. Her head was fuzzy with it, and she knew that she would have been out for days without the implants.

The curtain twitched, and a woman in a teal uniform peeked around the edge. She smiled to see the patient awake, and held up a finger in front of her lips to signal that she should remain quiet. The curtain fell back into place as the woman disappeared, and Tuya heard her approach the guards and talk softly with them. She strained to make out the conversation, but the hum and beeps of machines in the room crowded out the voices.

Several minutes later the woman returned, pushing past the edge of the curtain and holding a tray with instruments and syringes. She set the tray down on the rolling table placed near the bed, and then turned to face Tuya.

"My name is Jen," she whispered, placing a hand on Tuya's. "A group of us are working with your crew to get off the *Indomitable*. I can't go into the plan now, but I need you to trust me and be ready to move when I give you the signal. Can you do that?"

Tuya stared into the woman's green eyes, searching for any deception. She could see a familiar pain in them, that of terrible loss, and decided that she had no choice but to trust and hope it was not a ruse. She nodded her assent.

Jen patted her hand, turning to grab a large syringe. The woman placed the needle into a port on the line that connected Tuya to an IV bag, and pushed the plunger to inject the solution into the flow. Tuya's eyes widened at the betrayal, and she reached across to yank out the IV line.

She found that the needle was no longer inserted into the veins on top of her hand, however. The solution was instead leaking out onto the plastic surface of the bed and being soaked up by her blankets. She looked up at Jen to receive a wink, relaxing with the knowledge that her trust was well placed so far.

After leaving the curtained-off area, she heard Jen call out to the guards that the solution would take effect within half an hour and that the doctor would arrive shortly after for the operation. Tuya sensed that whatever was expected would happen before that time, and she started to slowly tighten her muscles for a few seconds at a time to ensure that her body would be ready to move. The grogginess of the sedatives was still strongly affecting her, and she knew that even a half second of slowness could be disastrous in a fight.

She heard the faint hiss of the main doors opening and then closing about twenty minutes later. The guards gave a surprised greeting to whoever entered, and asked why they were there. A cocky voice replied, moving as the speaker stepped farther into the room, and then she heard the noises of a fight. Tuya was about to rise from her bed and rush out to help what she assumed was a rescue, but the scuffle was soon finished.

The curtain around her bed was retracted on its rail, revealing two marines standing over two other marines on the floor. She was concerned that the wrong side had won the fight, until Jen stepped up with a smile.

"These are my friends, Tom and Richard. Hop out of the bed, and we'll get the guards hidden here."

Tuya rolled to her feet, standing on unsteady legs and suddenly grateful that her assistance had not been needed in the fight. The two men Jen had introduced quickly stripped the armor and bio suits off the unconscious guards, before pulling them onto the bed and arranging them as best as they could under the covers to look like one sleeping person. It was an illusion that would only fool those who weren't paying much attention. Jen injected each with a sedative to ensure that they didn't wake until their plan was complete.

"Okay, you two get suited up," the one she thought was Tom said. "The bio suits should fit pretty well, but the armor plating will be a little big. You just need to look passable, though, so that'll work."

"How long do we have?" the other man asked as the women stripped down and started to get into the marine gear.

"The doctor is a lazy bastard, so I fully expect he won't show up for at least an hour to make sure he can leave right after the scheduled operation's completed." Jen struggled to stretch the bio suit material over her large bust, and could then zip everything up. "One of the nurses will probably be here in half an hour to prep, but I don't think they'll check on the patient. Everyone around here seems to assume I'm the only one that should do the grunt work."

"That works out great for us," probably Tom said. He was keeping his eyes averted from the women while they changed, but Tuya noted that the other man openly watched the process with a joyful glint in his eye. Her scowl did nothing to turn away his gaze.

Buckling the last strap on her chest plating, Tuya was feeling the grogginess subside and her energy return. She helped Jen with her armor, grateful for her own smaller breasts when she saw how the other woman's chest piece had to be tilted to leave a large gap over her stomach.

"They couldn't have put at least one female guard on the duty roster today," Jen grumbled as she tried to adjust the hard plating and failed.

"Sorry," the jerk who had to be Richard replied. "The women on our shift are up on bridge duty today."

"What are we doing?" Tuya asked, tired of being left out of the loop on the plans.

"Getting you out of here, for a start." She was sure now that he was Tom. She liked him immediately, but had doubts about the other man. "We need to get through a lot of corridors and down several levels, so stick close and try to copy our posture. If we do pass another patrol, they should focus on me and Richard and just glance at the two of you behind us."

"I'll fill you in on the plan while we walk," Jen told her.

The group left the medical bay after checking the corridor was clear, and began the long trek. As they walked, Jen whispered of the nighttime conference between groups and roughly outlined the plan that they had come up with. At Altan's behest, she left out his name and that of their ship. He wanted to be the one to break the news of his survival.

"Isaac came up with all of this?" Tuya asked in disbelief at the end of the recitation.

"He had the broad strokes, and the rest of us filled them in with more details based on our experiences. Working on the crew of the ship the last few years has given me and my friends a good idea of the weaknesses of the routines."

"I owe all of you a great debt. If that operation had happened, I don't know that I would have wanted to live much longer."

Jen placed a reassuring hand on her wrist, then stiffened as a couple of off-duty crew members appeared farther down the corridor. Both women tried to make themselves appear taller, knowing that their slightness would make it hard for them to pass as men without the camouflage of Richard and Tom in front of them. The face shields of their helmets were down to keep all but their mouths hidden behind the dark visor. The boisterous pair approached, laughing over some joke and clearly on the way to inebriation.

The woman in the duo whistled loudly. "I've always loved a man in uniform, and here we have a group of fine specimens."

Tuya grimaced, keeping her eyes forward and marching in step with the men in front of her. They silently passed the off-duty crew, and it shocked her to feel a hard pat on her bottom as she walked by. Laughter erupted behind, and it receded as the duo continued on their way.

"We're almost there," Tom said quietly, as they entered the lift to make the descent. It was empty of other occupants, and she was grateful for the low number of crew on the ship. If there had been even a quarter of the full complement a ship like this would carry, the corridors would have been crowded with men and women carrying out tasks or returning to cabins for rest between shifts.

It had taken half an hour to reach their destination, and time was growing short before Tuya's absence from the medical bay would be noticed. Tom held out a hand to bring the group to a stop as they approached an intersection, and leaned forward to take a quick look.

"Still only two guards on the door," he whispered. "Richard and I are going to see if we can distract them the way we did the guards in medical. If you hear us call out, come running." He glanced at the women to make sure they acknowledged the plan, and then pulled a flechette pistol out of a low-slung holster and passed it over to Jen. "Don't hesitate to shoot them if you have to."

"They'd do the same to me, I know," Jen replied with her lips in a tight line.

The men stepped around the corner and sauntered down the corridor. Tuya could hear one of them call out a friendly greeting, met with an answering growl. She slid down the wall and then leaned over to peek around the corner at a height where she would be less noticeable. Tom was standing a few feet from the guards, trying to engage them in conversation while Richard moved nonchalantly past them. The guards were not in a friendly mood, however, barking out an order to be on their way.

She watched Tom take a step closer, and the guard nearest him pulled their weapon and centered it on his chest. Tom raised his hands, and tried to talk the guard down.

Richard, meanwhile, had made his way to the other side of the group and was in a perfect position to attack from behind. He planted his feet, however, and casually placed his hands behind his back in a resting position. "The implant freak is around the corner with the orderly," he told the guards as Tom looked at him in shocked betrayal.

"What the hell?" Jen breathed as Tuya ducked back from the corner. They heard Tom ask what was going on, and then the sound of a stun pistol shooting a dart. Soon followed by his collapse to the ground.

"Come out," Richard called to the two women. "There are patrols converging on this area now, so you have nowhere to go."

"How could you do this?" Jen called out, her voice wavering with shock and fear.

"Are you kidding?" Richard replied disdainfully. "There is no way a guild freighter could ever get away from a warship. One railgun blast, and that freighter would be scrap floating through the belt with our bodies. I went to the Commander to confess our plan while Tom thought I was involved in a tryst. Guildersen promised to promote me and make me a full member of the squad."

"You bastard!" Jen yelled back. "You turned your back on friends close enough to be family just for a promotion?"

"Better to be a part of the winning side than one of the casualties of the war." His tone had a hint of mocking laughter in it, an arrogant cockiness.

Tuya ground her teeth and took another quick peek around the corner. Two more helmeted marines had exited the cabin, and all four had their weapons drawn and pointed in her direction while Richard stood unarmed as he talked. She felt the anger flood her body, and turned to the woman beside her. "Give me the gun."

Jen willingly passed the weapon over, shoulders slumped in defeat. Tuya had no such doubts, however, and thumped the woman's chest plate to grab her attention.

"I need you to listen. When I'm engaged, you need to check on Tom. Make sure he's still alive, and get him out of the danger area. If you can grab a weapon and help out, that would be great." Jen nodded morosely, and Tuya gritted her teeth. She took a few deep breaths to steady herself. "Now ask him about the others."

Jen furrowed her brow in confusion, but followed the command and yelled out the question. "What about the rest of the *Vagabond* crew? And our friends?"

Richard barked out a cynical laugh. "Those idiots are in the cabin, and Mira's with them. As for...."

He broke off as Tuya rounded the corner and sprinted down the corridor. She raised the flechette pistol and pulled the trigger as quickly as she could, one of the marines going down in a heap as the others ducked down and raised their weapons to return fire. Stun bolts passed within inches of her twisting body, and she heard the hum of lethal flechette rounds passing by as well. With a grim smile, she jumped up to spring off the wall and flip over the group to land behind them. As they turned to face her, she put a round through the faceplate of the closest marine.

The remaining two troopers fired at the same time, a stun bolt impacting her chest plate while a flechette round passed through a weak point at her shoulder. Tuya leaped forward to kick the gun out of the hands of one marine, and followed up by grabbing the man's helmet to give it a brutal twist. Releasing her hold on the dead man, she reached out to grab Richard's wrist as he was finally moving to draw his weapon. She snapped the bones with a quick jerk, and then pulled him close and turned him to use as a shield against the final marine. That man looked down at his stun pistol, then looked back up at her with fear in his eyes.

She raised her pistol to point it at him and pulled the trigger. A dry click signaled that the weapon was out of rounds, and she tossed the pistol at the marine. He raised an arm to deflect the missile, only to be surprised as Tuya swung a yelping Richard around in a circle and released him to collide with the marine. Tuya sprinted forward to grab the stunned marine, flipping him around and wrapping her arm around his neck above the chest plate as she held him tight against her body. The man struggled in her grasp, his hands ineffectually trying to pry loose her grip, but she held on with enhanced strength as he struggled to get air. She smiled down into the wide eyes of the traitor as she choked the life from the last marine, dropping his lifeless body after a long silence.

Tuya stepped toward Richard as he tried to crawl away in a panic. "Please," he said. "Don't hurt me. I didn't mean it. They forced me to do it. I swear!"

She said nothing, only smiled wider as she advanced on him.

"Wait," a croaking voice called out. She looked up to see Tom leaning on Jen as they stood nearby. "I know the bastard deserves it, but he's my friend. We'll restrain him in the cabin. Let him explain how he failed to stop us from getting away. The Commander will punish him more than we ever could."

Tuya considered the request, kneeling over the traitor as he lay before her. She grabbed his chest plate, pulling his torso up off the floor, and tilted her head to examine the wretched looking man. "Okay," she finally said.

Hope blossomed in his eyes, and then blinked out as she raised a fist and with a lightning strike knocked him unconscious. She dragged his limp body to the side of the corridor, retrieving restraints from one of the dead troopers and binding his hands and feet. Then she stepped across and slapped the button to open the cabin door, moving quickly into the room at a crouch and scanning for any hostile troopers.

"Tuya!" she heard Erik call out from the bunks where he, Isaac, and Fynn were sitting with their hands cuffed behind their backs. A woman sat with them, who she assumed to be Mira.

Jen and Tom entered the cabin behind her, the marine being escorted to sit in a chair so that Jen could get a better look at the small stun bolt that was lodged in his shoulder between armor pieces.

"Where are the others?" Mira asked, looking toward the cabin door as Tuya moved to cut away the restraints from the four prisoners.

"Richard turned on us," Tom said through grunts as the bolt was pulled out, looking over at his former friend's slumped form. "The bastard traded us all in for a chance to be one of *them.*"

"What about Altan?" Fynn inquired. "Do we know if he succeeded in his part of the plan?"

Tuya turned sharply at the name. "Who? Did you say Altan?"

EIGHTEEN

Erik massaged his wrists; the rough plastic restraints had rubbed his skin raw with the slightest movement and left several bloody spots. When the marines had entered the cabin half an hour before, pushing Mira before them already restrained, he had felt all of his hopes fade away. Somehow the Syndicate had figured out what the freighter crews were trying to do, or at least the part that Mira played. The marines had not spoken a word while in the cabin, only restrained everyone and then waited for the signal which sent them scrambling out into the corridor.

He had been delighted to see Tuya, looking a bit battered but otherwise as unshakeable as always. That joy was diminished in learning that one of their group had betrayed them, but knowing the source of the Syndicate's information was better than worrying at how they had screwed up. The small number of marines on board the cruiser was the only thing that had kept them from laying a trap with overwhelming numbers. He had a feeling that the commander who sent them had also underestimated the danger that Tuya presented. If the operating system had reached the

Vagabond, then they still had a very good chance at success.

"Did you say Altan?" he heard, shaking him from his reverie.

"Tuya," he said gently. "Your brother is alive. These people are survivors from *Telemachus*, captured like us and forced to join the Syndicate crew to stay alive."

He saw disbelief flash across her face, followed by joy and then sadness. "I gave up," she whispered. "I gave up, when I should have fought to keep looking for him."

Erik stepped forward and put an arm around her shoulders. "You had no way of knowing. The Syndicate staged the destruction of the ship in a place it would be found specifically so that no one would look for it or the crew."

"We need to move!" Tom ordered, grabbing up dropped weapons in the corridor to hand them out to the rest of the group. "More troopers are on the way, and they'll arrive at any minute. The plan to get everyone into marine armor and sneak aboard the *Vagabond* is over."

"Altan," Tuya said wondrously, then looked around at the others. "Where is he? What was he doing?"

"I got a message from him right before they grabbed me," Mira spoke up, checking the stun pistol she was holding to count the available rounds. "He'd finished the software download and initiated the install on *Vagabond*."

"He should be here, then. Right?" Tuya asked urgently.

"No, he'll still be working his shift with the maintenance crew. They're working near the freighter, though, so the plan called for us to alert him when we approached the ship so he could slip away and get on board."

"He's not working his shift," Tom said from the corridor. The rest of the group left the cabin to gather around him, where he was tapping at a wrist terminal taken off one of the dead marines. "They killed my access to the system, but I was able pull up reports here. They grabbed Altan shortly after they got Mira." He looked up at them with stricken eyes. "He's in a cell, guarded by half a squad of marines."

There was a long silence, and they all glanced at Tuya. Her expression grew grimmer with each word Tom spoke, and now the anger was plainly written across her face. "Where is he?"

"The detention cells are on the opposite side of the ship," Tom said apologetically. "It would take half an hour at least to get there, and it's the most heavily trafficked part of the ship."

Erik placed a hand on her harm, unconsciously trying to restrain her. "We can't get him out, but we can still escape and make sure everyone knows what the Syndicate is doing and that he's being held prisoner."

Tuya turned stormy eyes on him, and he took an involuntary step back. "I'm not leaving my brother, Frost. Not again. Not ever."

"We don't have time for this," Mira said quietly, facing down the corridor. "I can hear people coming. It's time to move, and we have to get to the freighter or we'll never escape."

"I'm not leaving him," Tuya asserted. She pulled a flechette gun from Tom's hand, bending down to retrieve an extra clip of rounds from the body at her feet. As she was straightening back up, four marines rounded the corner at the intersection and came to a surprised stop.

"Down on the ground!" one of the troopers yelled, as they all raised stun pistols at the group. Tom fired immediately, hitting a marine high in the neck with a stun bolt that sent the man into convulsions. His overstimulated muscles caused his limbs to flail, knocking another marine to the ground as the others opened fire.

Erik ducked back into the cabin, herding Isaac and Fynn behind him. Once behind cover, he looked at the weapon he had been given to see that he carried a lethal flechette pistol. He leaned carefully around the door to get a view on the marines assaulting the group, and pointed the pistol down the corridor. Pulling the trigger repeatedly, he reflected that he would need to train with firearms if they made it out of this situation. He watched his shots go wide, but finally dialed in on his target. The last round in the clip hit the marine, but lodged in the chest plate and seemed to not faze the man at all.

"I'm out!" he called, ducking back into the cabin and turning to his friends. Fynn was holding out the stun pistol he had been handed, and Erik grabbed it gratefully. He looked out to see Tom and Tuya both shielding themselves behind the dead troopers. Jen and Mira had retreated down the corridor and found an unlocked room to take cover in. All four were firing at the advancing marines.

He leaned out into the corridor, seeing a second marine down while the one who had been knocked down earlier was now walking forward. Taking careful aim at one of the advancing marines, he pulled the trigger twice in quick succession to send bolts flying down the hall. The first bounced off an armor plate, but the second found a gap and the voltage sent the trooper into debilitating convulsions before she dropped unconscious.

With only one enemy left, he saw Tuya stand from her cover and run at the marine with a scream of rage. The man's eyes widened in shock just before she pounced and they tumbled to the ground. Erik could hear solid sounds of blows hitting flesh and armor plating, and left the cover of the cabin to assist his friend in the fight. He found her sitting triumphantly on top of the incapacitated marine, pulling a flechette pistol and clip from the man's belt.

"More will be coming," Tom said, scanning the salvaged terminal. "Another full squad was sent out about ten minutes ago."

Erik nodded his understanding, approaching Tuya. "We need to get to the *Vagabond*. The people on this ship are going to kill millions if we don't warn Earth and the colonies."

"I'm not leaving Altan, Frost." The woman turned to look at him, and he could see that her anger had softened. "Go. Take the others, get to the ship, and get away from here."

He stared at her, trying to understand. "I can't leave you behind," he said with a strained voice.

"You can, and you will." Tuya stood and walked over to grab him in a crushing hug. "Thank you for being such a great captain, and for getting me here to help my brother. I'll never forget you, Frost." She looked over his shoulder at the group standing further down the corridor. "Any of you." Without another word, she turned and ran back the way she had come from the medical bay, disappearing around the corner.

Erik stood gaping, looking at the empty corridor where she had been. He had known Tuya to be brave and confident from the first moment that he met her, but he was only now understanding what true courage and loyalty was. He said a silent prayer that she made it to her brother, and turned to the rest of the group with a sigh.

"Lead the way, Tom. Let's get to the *Vagabond* and get off this monstrosity."

"She left us," Isaac was whispering over and over.

Erik walked over to grab the tech with a reassuring hand. "She had to do it, Isaac. Not just for Altan, but for herself. She didn't leave us. She just took a different path."

The group ran quickly through twisting corridors, making their way to the airlock where the freighter was docked. Poking a head around a corner, Tom reported that there were two marines standing guard.

"Should have grabbed more rounds," Erik said, looking down at the empty flechette gun he was still carrying.

Isaac held out the stun pistol he had been carrying, and Tom grabbed it quickly. Jen reported that she still had a few bolts left in the weapon she carried. Leading the way, Tom and Jen stepped out into the corridor and fired at the marines standing in the airlock antechamber. Luck led one of the bolts to incapacitate a trooper right away, while the second turned to face the threat and began to return fire.

Erik leaned around the corner to throw his two expended weapons at the trooper several meters away. The distraction was enough for Jen's last shot to find a mark. With both troopers down, they rushed ahead into the antechamber. Their luck turned sour as they found the airlock hatch locked down and the terminal next to it completely dark.

"They disabled the airlock," Tom said in disgust, punching at the wall. "The only way to open it is from the bridge controls."

"Let me take a look," Isaac said, pushing through the group to examine the terminal. He ran his hands along the bulkhead around the screen, grunting as he seemed to find what he was looking for. "I need a screwdriver, or a knife with a thin blade."

Jen reached into a pocket of her uniform, pulling out a small scalpel. "Will this work?"

"That should do it," Isaac confirmed, taking the implement with a bashful smile. He worked the blade into a small groove, and then applied pressure to pop the panel cover loose enough to get a finger under the edge. Once the panel was free, he set it aside and examined the exposed wiring around the terminal. He passed the scalpel back to Jen.

Erik raised an eyebrow as she slipped the small blade back into a pocket. "Do you always carry that thing around?"

"It was the only weapon I could explain away if the marines ever saw it," she explained. "I feel exposed on this ship if I don't have at least one way to defend myself."

Mira chuckled, and pulled a small leather ball from her own pocket. "It's filled with ball bearings," she explained. "I tell people it's a stress ball if they ask, but when I hold it in my fist I can deliver a good punch." The women shared a laugh, and Erik was about to speak when Isaac called out triumphantly.

"Found it. I just have to attach this wire to this connector...." The group saw the terminal flicker and the display came to life.

"You bypassed the security system?" Jen asked, stepping over to look at the wiring with interest.

"It wasn't too hard," Isaac replied with a blush. "The people who install the technical systems always put in a few backdoor ways to circumvent things like a security lockdown. Too often, it's done by accident or someone who shouldn't be doing it."

Jen smiled at the tech, which just made his face turn a deeper shade of crimson. "Easy for you, but impossible for the rest of us to figure out."

Tom coughed, and stepped between the two. "How about we pop this hatch, now that we have the controls back?" He tapped on the screen to pull up the menu and then started the cycle to pressurize and open the airlock. The group waited for the process to complete, several of them looking back down the corridor from time to time to make sure it was still clear.

When the airlock door swung open, the group piled into the tight interior that was made for three or four at a time, not six. They tried to avoid groping the others in the crush, waiting as the door closed and the computer verified the air pressure in the docking tunnel was stable. As soon as that process completed, they filed into the tube and hustled across to the freighter. Erik took the lead, enabling him to enter his security code on the ship's terminal.

He was entering the last digit as Tom called out from the back of the group. "Get in the ship. A squad of marines is advancing down the corridor! I see them clearing the rooms, but they'll be at the airlock in minutes."

Erik shoved through into the *Vagabond*'s airlock, pressing the button to open the inner door. "Come on, come on," he said under his breath, impatiently waiting as the freighter's computer ran the same air integrity check that they'd waited through on the other side of the docking tunnel. Seconds passed slowly, until he finally heard the click that announced that the locks were released and he was able to push the hatch open.

"They're in the antechamber," Tom yelled.

"Everyone into the ship," Fynn said, waving people through the airlock into the freighter. "I'll detach the docking collar as soon as we get in."

"It takes almost ten minutes for the computer to run the undocking process at the best of times," Isaac complained. "Those marines will be in our airlock cutting through the door by then."

"I'm going to do this fast and messy," the engineer replied. "We'll have to put in to a shipyard for repairs before we can dock with anything again, but I think it's worth it in this case."

"Agreed," Erik told him as Tom leaped into the freighter. "Do it, and let me know when we're ready to move." He could see the marines already inside the *Indomitable*'s airlock, running the air integrity cycle before they could spill out into the tube.

He rushed through the corridors of his ship, lovingly running a hand along bulkheads that he had feared he would never get to see again. Isaac was escorting the newcomers in the opposite direction, getting them ensconced in whatever crash couches were available, but Mira was on his heels as he entered the control room.

"Take the pilot's station," he told her, noting the longing look in her eyes as she entered the room and saw the three seats. With a joyful grin, she settled into the chair and deftly booted up the terminals in front of her.

Erik felt the same exultation as he settled into the old command chair, tapping the button to power up the station without hesitation. The operating system that had been loaded into the ship was a vast improvement over the makeshift programs they had been running on for most of a month. The terminals booted up quickly to display status reports that were all in the green. Tentatively, he pressed the button for the holo displays and gave out a cry of joy as they flickered into existence in front of his eyes and on the main display that all three stations could view.

The engines were in the process of warming up, and the ship's reactor was out of standby mode after more than a day of minimal usage. He pulled up the ion thruster display, and was grateful to see that he would have access to over eighty percent of their full power.

"How's everything looking?" he asked, turning toward the pilot's station.

"All systems green, and this old clunker is ready to fly," Mira replied. He could hear the smile in her voice, and he wondered how long it would last now that she was back in a pilot's chair for the first time in almost a decade.

Erik flicked the switch for the ship's intercom. "Are we ready, Fynn?"

"Ready, captain. Punch it."

"You heard the man. Get us out of here as fast as we can go."

"Aye, captain." Mira's hands flew across the console tapping in commands and pulling up the thruster controls. The ship shuddered as she maneuvered it away from the bulk of the Syndicate cruiser, and once she was comfortable with the space between the vessels she threw the ion thrusters into a six G burn. A long black streak of burned hull plating was left along the side of the cruiser, the freighter's engines too close to the ship when they flared to life.

Erik was pushed back in his couch, and was happy to see that the four people outside the control room were safely ensconced to ride out the acceleration. He flipped his display to the camera outside the airlock, unable to resist a chuckle at the sight of a squad of marines floating away from where the docking tunnel had been ripped off the *Vagabond*'s docking collar. A small part of him felt bad about the death of the men and women, but he knew they would have been happy to kill or maim any or all of his group.

"Captain, the *Indomitable* is increasing power to her own thrusters. They're moving to overtake us." Mira put the view of the warship onto the main display, and they watched as ion engines half the size of the freighter flared to propel the ship.

"The railguns!" he exclaimed, seeing movement around one of the emplacements on the side of the ship facing the freighter. The nearest gun fired, the round passing several hundred meters away from the freighter. Another railgun farther back on the cruiser's flank fired, this round passing by on the other side of the *Vagabond*.

"We're in the sweet spot," Mira said with an audible grin. "The functional railguns are too far apart and can't rotate enough to hit something of our size in this position." As she spoke, the guns continued to fire impotently.

"We'll have to pass through those firing lanes to get away from the ship. Can you make our course erratic enough to elude the guns?"

"I can, cap, but it's going to be a pretty wild ride."

Erik said a brief prayer, and took a deep breath. "Everyone hang on. This will get a little rough."

He flicked off the intercom and made sure one of his main screens displayed the medical stats for everyone in the crash couches. "Do whatever it takes, Mira. I don't care if you need to push us past the G force safety limits, just get us out of their range."

"Aye, cap."

Erik pulled up the communications system, running a quick diagnostic to ensure that the new operating system was working properly with the *Vagabond*'s antenna arrays. The small test packet showed as successfully sent out, and he started to set up an outgoing message marked for broadcast across all the public communication bandwidths. With the ship moving wildly through turns as tight as Mira could make them, he turned on the video camera pointed at his station and recorded the message.

"I'm Erik Frost, captain of the guild freighter *Vagabond*. My crew and I accepted a job several months ago to deliver cargo to a so-called black site." He tapped a button that would insert a picture of the misshapen cargo container into the message for a few seconds.

"The main stipulation of the job was that our AI had to control the ship to and from the delivery location. Due to a malfunction in our ship's AI, our ship was nearly disabled and working with jury-rigged systems when we arrived at the rendezvous point. What we found there was a Syndicate war ship larger than anything yet constructed." Another button, to display an image of the ship captured by the exterior cameras as they raced away from it.

"Once docked, my crew and I were taken into custody to protect the secret of the vessel, called *Indomitable*. While imprisoned, we met the remainder of the crew of the freighter *Telemachus*, which disappeared seven years ago. That ship had carried the same kind of cargo, the crew managed to get a glimpse of the warship, and the Syndicate admiral had the *Telemachus* destroyed. The crew was given a choice of joining the Syndicate crew or death, and they all reluctantly chose to join. During their years working on the vessel, they learned of the planned mission once construction was complete. The Syndicate will use the heavy cruiser to destroy the Mars scientific outposts, and then the Coalition dome on Luna. Coalition cities on Earth will be targeted until that government folds."

Erik paused to let the words sink in for whoever heard this message.

"Thanks to the brave assistance of the remaining *Telemachus* crew, we have managed to escape and are fleeing now. If you get this message, please send it on to everyone you can. We need to make sure that Earth sees this warning and prepares. The *Indomitable* is lightly armed at the moment, and operating with a skeleton crew. She is vulnerable to a concerted attack by multiple frigates, but that will not last if the admiral manages to gather more weapons and crew. Please, help us save millions of lives."

He looked into the camera for several seconds, trying to think of a stronger appeal, and then reached over to end the message. "Are we outside their jamming field yet?"

"Almost," Mira responded, hands still flying across the controls as she kept the freighter moving erratically. "A few more minutes and we should have pulled away enough."

Erik considered the movements, brow furrowing. They had been fleeing from the cruiser for a quarter of an hour, and the sudden silence started to register on him. "When did they stop firing at us?" he mused aloud.

"About five minutes ago. A few of the rounds came close, but thanks to having the best freighter pilot in the system aboard we managed to avoid them."

He shook his head, though Mira couldn't see it. "They have torpedoes. One of those could lock in and catch us no matter what maneuvers we went through.

Two if they wanted to be sure of the kill. Not to mention the fighters and assault shuttles that could have been launched to chase after us." He flipped the intercom switch. "Guys, why would the *Indomitable* not be giving their full effort to chasing us?"

"I think I know," Jen chimed in. "Guildersen was in the med bay several weeks back, and I heard him talking with the doctor. It sounded like he was unhappy about having to hide away in the asteroid belt, convinced that the ship was already strong enough to join the Syndicate frigates and overwhelm the Coalition fleet. I think the admiral may have been feeling the pressure to make a move for a long while."

"That could be it," Tom conceded. "One of the marine lieutenants has mentioned several times that Guildersen was making waves with the command staff, convinced that we were being wasted out here. Having the existence of the *Indomitable* exposed will force the military committee on Earth to finally act."

Erik grimaced at the thought that he might have inadvertently started the process that he was hoping to expose and put an early end to. "Mira, let's get out of range of the signal jamming as quick as possible."

"Aye, captain." She ceased the erratic movements, angling the freighter on an oblique from the cruiser. They pulled farther away, and the *Indomitable* made no move to turn and follow.

His stomach dropped as he pulled up a projected path of the cruiser. The dotted line turned into a cone of probability on the displayed map, but the colony on

Interamnia was in the center of that path. If the freighter had carried a weapon of any kind, even an old-fashioned machine gun emplacement, he would have ordered an attack to try and assuage the guilt and anger he felt.

"We're clear!" Mira called out, and he saw the communication status switch over to green. Erik tapped urgently to send the video out, and watched the display until it reported a successful transmission. The file was shooting across space to multiple asteroid colonies, to Mars, to Luna, even to people on Earth that would receive the message on the public bands. He could only hope it would spur the action needed to save Interamnia.

NINETEEN

Lieutenant Davis marched onto the quarterdeck of the cruiser, pausing for a moment to examine the view in the large displays surrounding the pit below where crew members were hard at work. It felt liberating to see the ship moving through the starfield once more, and know that they were finally on the way to begin their mission.

He stopped several paces away from where Admiral Yumata was leaning on the rail of the quarterdeck, a small area a level higher than the rest of the bridge where senior officers could gather. Commander Guildersen stood nearby, his posture stiff as he spoke with the admiral.

"I ordered the gunners to cease firing because we both know it's time that the system knew of our existence, admiral. This freighter can do nothing to us, but we can use them to force Earth into moving against the Coalition once and for all."

Yumata shook his head slowly. "I'm disappointed that you would impose your view of the situation on the rest of us in this manner. We have discussed this many times, and I feel that I made my opinion on the matter clear."

"Yes, admiral, but I have a different opinion. Mine is shared by several members of the executive committee. They've sent me messages many times over the last year asking how much longer they would have to keep pretending to the military stalemate."

The admiral sighed, and finally turned to face the man who was supposed to serve as his right hand on board the cruiser. "Well, the system will soon know of our existence now. We have no choice but to begin our advance on the home world."

Guildersen smiled and Davis could see his chins almost wobble with a ripple of pleasure. "Shall I give the order to burn for Mars, admiral?"

Yumata shook his head. "No, if we are going to be exposed so soon, then we must make a quick impression. Continue on for that colony on Interamnia. Let us show the Coalition how dangerous the *Indomitable* can be, even when lightly armed."

Davis couldn't believe what he was hearing, but kept himself from betraying his shock through his rigid posture. As one of the admiral proteges, he had been privy to the man's private thoughts over the years. He knew that Yumata was not the bloodthirsty warrior that he sometimes pretended to be.

Guildersen was too full of glee to wonder about the orders at all, as he laboriously stepped onto the small lift that would carry him down to the main bridge deck below. The machinery seemed to groan beneath his weight.

"Lieutenant, I hear that the freighter crew you vouched for has managed to kill two squads of our marines."

Davis stepped forward and presented a crisp salute to the admiral's back. "Yes, sir, with another squad injured. I admit that I underestimated them when they were brought on board."

"You allowed yourself to get too close," Yumata said, turning dark eyes on the soldier. "The Commander wanted you stripped of your rank as an example for the rest of the crew, but I have overruled him. Now that we are beginning our mission to take control of the system, I will need you and your recon troops more than ever."

The admiral turned back to look over the mostly empty stations below, hands clasped at the small of his back. "Ramp up your training, lieutenant. We will not need you for this show of force on the mining colony, but your team will be called on soon."

"Yes, admiral." Davis saluted again, before turning sharply and marching from the quarterdeck. He took a curving stairway to the main bridge deck, where he could see Commander Guildersen laughing with one of the marines on guard duty. He turned to leave through a different door, placing a call for his sergeant as he left the bridge.

TWENTY

After an hour of flying away from the Syndicate cruiser without any sign of it changing course to follow, Erik ordered Mira to drop their speed long enough to allow everyone to climb into high gravity suits. He watched the cruiser pass them by and continue deeper into the belt, and his anger grew as he considered the atrocities that the crew on board would gladly participate in.

Once they were all suited up and strapped back in, Mira punched the power to the engines and the ion thrusters flared with a burst of speed that brought to mind the wild ride when the AI had taken them away from the colony they were now desperate to get back to. Aside from the thousands of oblivious people, two of the ship's crew were stranded there and Erik was willing to put the safety of his ship and self at risk to rescue them.

He watched as the increased acceleration thrust pushed the readings over ten G's, maxing out the capacity of the engines with the current operating system. He fought against the strain on his body to type in a quick message on the keypad near his fingertips before sending it to display on all terminal screens on the ship. *Three hours of high thrust, then a break.*

Despite the short reduction in thrust to get everyone into high gravity suits, they were able to pull alongside the *Indomitable* near the end of the high burn. There was a five hundred kilometer gap between the two vessels, which was as close as Erik felt it was safe to be in case the cruiser veered in their direction to try and fire at them again. It surprised him to see that the Syndicate ship was still increasing speed, and it edged away again just before Mira reduced the thrust to allow everyone a breather from the heavy strain.

"What is the max speed on that ship?" he asked the pilot.

"From the reports and engine tests I experienced on the bridge, the *Indomitable* can travel comfortably at the same ten Gs that we are pushing up to." She turned her chair around to look him in the eye with a determined look. "Don't kid yourself, cap. They are going to reach whatever destination they have in mind well before we could. With the high powered reactors onboard and suspension gel pods for the purpose, that ship can get to twenty Gs within a few hours of constant acceleration."

Erik shut his eyes tightly, feeling all hope that had built up crushed by the simple statement. A faint ping from his terminal drew his attention and he opened one eye to find a message waiting indicator flashing. He scrambled to bring up his inbox, and found a few responses waiting to the video message he had sent out.

Message received, the first said, sent from the colony on Cybele. *Please verify your identity and send transponder reading of possible enemy vessel.* He couldn't believe that such a direct threat would be questioned, even from an anonymous sender account. He sent out a quick reply that the Syndicate vessel was not transmitting a transponder code.

The second message had arrived shortly before they dropped out of the acceleration thrust and came from Interamnia. He opened the file to find a video message from the colony administrator, Agatha. "Captain Frost, your message has sparked panic here. Most of the administrative council refuse to believe your warning and demand verification before we act. Please update us as soon as you can with any data you have."

Erik shook his head in shock at how easily his warnings were being dismissed. He compiled the tracking data the *Vagabond* computer had collected since they escaped, and sent it along with course projections in response to Agatha. *Even if you can't make them believe me,* he wrote, *get as many people as you can deeper into the asteroid.*

He keyed in the twenty G thrust target for the cruiser, postulated that it could maintain that much power for as much as forty-eight hours straight, and had the computer run projections on when the two ships would arrive at Interamnia. He was crestfallen at the results.

"They'll reach the colony days before we can," he said to Mira.

"I'm sorry, Erik," she replied. "We've done all we can by sending the warning out. It is up to everyone else to respond in time to try and stop the *Indomitable* now."

"I was naïve," he said, angry at himself. "I thought if I got the message out, the system would rally together to fight off the threat. Instead, even someone who knows me is hesitant to act on the warning for fear that I'm manufacturing or inflating the threat."

"Your video should be hitting Luna and Earth soon. Hopefully the people there will be more responsive."

"If not, we escaped just to have front row seats to the deaths of millions and the end of any hopes of independent operations by the colonies or guild."

Late on the fourth day of the trip, messages from Interamnia were intercepted. Many had been sent wildly with no real destination, panicked pleas for help as the colonists saw the Syndicate cruiser approaching and embraced the earlier warnings. Erik grimly watched a handful of the video clips, but could stand it no longer and let the rest be captured by the computer and stored without being viewed.

The only exception was an official message sent out by the administrative council, the video taken of the seven members seated around a small table with looks of despair. Agatha sat in the center, and spoke to the camera with her hands folded on the table in front of her.

"This is Agatha Crisp, administrator of Interamnia. Our sensors have picked up readings of a massive war ship approaching at high speed, which will arrive here within minutes. This is undoubtedly the *Indomitable*, the Syndicate cruiser that Captain Frost's message warned us of. Like most of you, I'm sure, we did not fully believe the warning. I no longer hold such delusions. Please learn from our mistake. This feed will remain active and continue to transmit until the danger has passed or the recorder is destroyed."

He watched as the council remained seated in morose silence, seemingly accepting their fate. It was not long before an aide rushed into the room to say that the approaching ship had demanded the colony's surrender to the Syndicate. The council met this announcement with frowns, and only one of them seemed inclined to argue in favor of the surrender. Agatha stared down the recalcitrant member, and turned to the aide.

"Tell them we refuse to bow to their demands. Interamnia fought hard to become a free colony, and we will not give up our freedom to the first tyrant who approaches. The fact that they would threaten to fire upon a defenseless mining colony tells me all I need to know about their brand of leadership."

The aide left to deliver the message, and he saw a few of the other council members begin to look green about the gills. One of the younger men rose from the table and rushed from the room with a hand over his mouth, but Agatha did not register the movement at all. Voices could be heard in the background, yelling in panic or rage, and occasionally people would run past the door of the room captured on video.

Agatha looked up at something above the camera lens, and her expression finally changed to an awed shock. "They're here," she whispered hoarsely. Moments later, the video stuttered and showed brief static before closing out. Erik looked at the now blank screen, crushed by the helplessness he felt.

"It could just be the jamming field that stopped the message," Mira spoke from the pilot's station. The video feed had been loud enough for her to hear though she could not see.

"Possibly. Hopefully. But I'm not sure I really believe it."

It took another three days to reach Interamnia with heavy burns for an hour each day before returning to cruising speed for their bodies and the ship to rest from the strain. Jen quickly took stock of the ship's medical bay and set about checking in with each of the five others during their rest periods to treat any bruising from blood pooling and a rib fracture on Fynn where his previous broken bone couldn't hold up under the strain.

Erik had continued sending messages to the colony since watching the ominous video feed Agatha had sent out on a wide spectrum transmission. None had received a response.

As they approached the location of the mining colony, hard braking burns slowed the ship enough to have a view of the area while maintaining enough speed for a hasty retreat if the Syndicate warship turned weapons on them. The freighter had been under so much stress in the last month that the rattles and shaking that had worried Erik for so many years had grown to a clamor that worried even Fynn. The hull fractures on the bow had begun to widen, but no one on the ship ever considered easing the strain and slowing their trip.

"Are the sensors picking up any sign of the *Indomitable?*" Erik asked once they were a few thousand kilometers from the asteroid.

"I'm not seeing any results indicative of it, captain." Mira flipped through several screens of sensor results. "We'll be in visual range shortly."

He sent the external bow camera feed to the main display, and they watched for the familiar shape of an asteroid that both of them had visited many times during contract runs.

"It should be right there," Erik said, pointing at an area of the screen that showed a familiar grouping of distant objects. He squinted as he examined the screen, glancing quickly at each object in the field of view and dismissing them as they didn't match the shape he was looking for.

"It's that one," Mira replied shakily. Her finger pointed toward a large asteroid in the lower left of the display. It was smaller and had a different shape than he remembered, and it took a few seconds for his mind to process what he was seeing. The docking tunnel gouged out during colonization was nowhere to be seen.

Instead, a huge chunk of the asteroid had been torn away to leave behind a massive crater with thousands of smaller rocks floating in a new orbit around what remained of Interamnia.

"Those bastards killed them all." Erik couldn't believe that he was seeing the destruction that meant hundreds of lives were cut short. The inventor, Robert, who had so proudly shown off his latest ideas would no longer dream up fascinating new projects. John and Sally Murphy, left behind by the out of control AI, would never again roam the corridors of the *Vagabond* and join the rest of the crew in friendly evenings in the galley or rec room. Agatha would never shamelessly flirt with Fynn again, conspiring with Erik to arrange meetings when the ship docked at the colony.

Everyone on board trickled into the control center, called in by Mira while he was lost in his thoughts. Isaac dropped into the navigator station and wept with Fynn standing at his side, a comforting hand draped over his shoulder. The *Telemachus* survivors huddled together near Mira, discussing the destruction of the colony in quiet voices. Erik looked around at all of them, three members remaining from the crews of each ship, gathered together in this moment of heartbreak and sorrow.

"We have all suffered great losses at the hands of the Syndicate. I for one can't sit back and just accept the deaths of friends and acquaintances, hoping that the boogeyman doesn't decide to turn around and come back for me. The *Vagabond* will not stand idle, but will take the fight to those who would crush anyone who opposes them. I am setting course for Luna in the hopes that we can lend aid in the fight, and also do everything in my power to rescue Tuya and Altan if they still live.

"Any of you who wish to join me are welcome. Those who wish to leave the ship as soon as we reach Luna are free to do so with no recriminations from me." He stopped, and looked at each occupant of the room. "Tom, Mira and Jen, I would be honored if you would join our crew and become a part of the *Vagabond* family."

"We'd be happy to be part of your crew, captain," Mira said. Tom and Jen added in their own assent.

"Excellent. Now, for the first order of business. Fynn, how do we go about mounting those undelivered railguns to give our freighter some bite?"

Erik was making his way through the messages that had been intercepted before the destruction of Interamnia, reading a handful each evening before exhaustion tossed him into sleep. He filed some away as reminders of the atrocity, and deleted others that were too hard to ever watch again. Midway through the list, he found a message from Robert.

Erik, it read, *I know that we may not have long here before the cruiser arrives. In the event that the worst comes to pass, I am entrusting to you all of my research and notes for fusion reactors. I have had a few breakthroughs since we last spoke, but there is still much research to be completed before this can become reality.   Make sure that someone continues the work, and put the end result to good use.   Robert.*

He chuckled as he read the note, looking at the dozens of attachments that were included, containing hundreds of gigabytes of data. He reminisced about the time he had spent listening to the inventor detail all the wonderful applications of the more powerful energy generating devices.

The smile slipped as his mind wandered to other uses for such devices. Uses that could give his ship and other guild freighters an edge over the Syndicate destroyer, and might provide a beacon of hope. He created a new video message, preparing to pass the information along to Dex so she could find trusted scientists to continue developing the new technology.

Vagabond was burning hard for the inner system, hoping to reach Earth before the Syndicate cruiser. Mira had reported that the ship seemed to be veering off to approach Mars first, despite the two planets drifting farther apart every day in their current orbits. Such a detour should give the freighter the time it needed to reach the home world before the cruiser.

Erik didn't like to think about what it could mean for the several hundred people living in the small facility on Deimos or working out of scientific outposts on the surface. He could only hope that the Coalition would send ships to try and protect those people, but the reactions so far hadn't been promising.   In the meantime, he was intent on working with the Transport Guild to do everything they could to help.

After two decades of sparring with words, the system was truly at war.

ACKNOWLEDGEMENTS

I would like to thank Bethany Wright for being a fantastic editor. She helped me identify the weak points in the early story, and gave me a ton of feedback on how I could improve the manuscript. This is my first book, and I know that it is ten times better than it was because of her assistance.

I'd also like to thank my family for putting up with my dreaming about being a writer for thirty years before actually sitting down and putting the first one down on paper.

Tim has been a dreamer since he was a small boy, finally putting all his wild imaginings onto paper.

During the day, he is an IT support technician for a nationwide bank. At night, he bangs away on his keyboard and often obsesses over the proper word to express an idea or feeling.

Visit him at www.timrangnow.com, where you can sign up for a newsletter to stay up to date on current and future projects. You'll also get early access to short stories and chapters of upcoming books.

Vagabond

Indomitable

Waterloo

Resolute

Made in the USA
Monee, IL
31 December 2021

87632973R00148